Eternal Paths

Christy Newton

CRIMSON ROMANCE™

F+W Media, Inc.

Published by
Crimson Romance™
an imprint of F+W Media, Inc.
10151 Carver Road, Suite 200
Blue Ash, OH 45242. U.S.A.
www.crimsonromance.com

ISBN 10: 1-5072-0012-9
ISBN 13: 978-1-5072-0012-4
eISBN 10: 1-5072-0013-7
eISBN 13: 978-1-5072-0013-1

Cover art © Shutterstock/Samot.

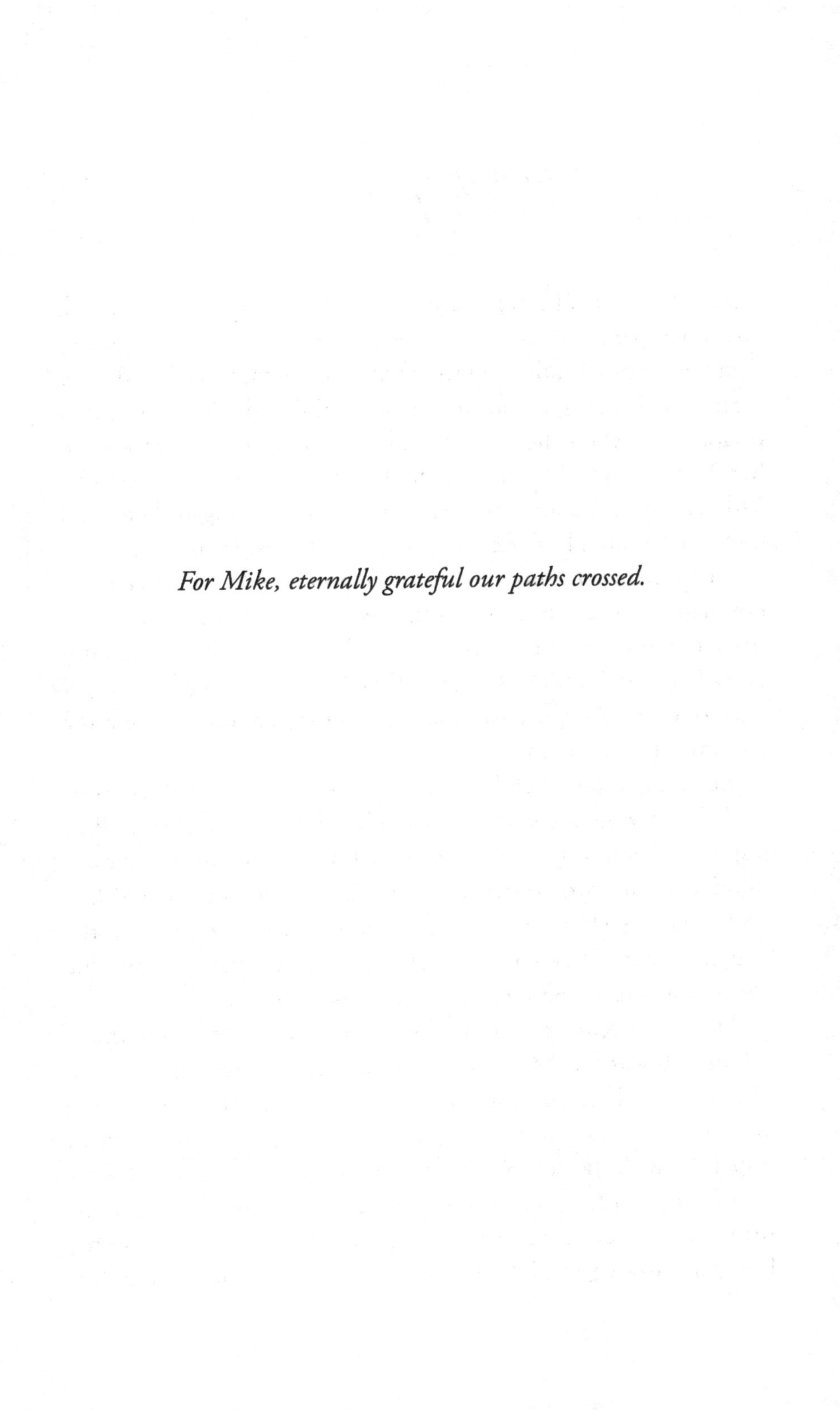

For Mike, eternally grateful our paths crossed.

Chapter 1

"Come back!" Hallie York gasped for air as she sprung up in bed. Sweat dampened her cotton tank top and panties. She struggled to come to terms with the nightmare of Frederick leaving her all over again. She hadn't seen her imaginary childhood friend since he'd disappeared when she started grade school. But there he was, in her dream, as vivid as the day she'd first imagined him. Frederick had been from London and had told her she belonged there with him. He'd visited her often and became her best friend.

Much to her parents' relief, as she'd gotten older, the imaginary boy had vanished, but her strong feelings for London had not. After Frederick left her, she'd gone to the library and checked out every book on London she could find. She tried everything to get him to return. As much as she'd tried to forget about him and the faraway city, she couldn't.

Being an adopted child, she'd never known her birth parents. And never would because of the closed adoption and Hallie's respect to honor it. She guessed her birth parents were from London ... that would explain a lot. The parents who raised her, both schoolteachers, never had the money to travel outside the United States. They couldn't have been better parents, but she constantly sensed something was missing from her life.

Hallie glanced at the clock. The alarm was set to go off in thirty minutes. It was finally time to see if London was the missing piece in her heart. Then, in three months, she could come back home and begin her dream career as a curator for the Smithsonian ... hopefully with the completeness she'd always been searching for.

After she took a quick shower, she put on her casual, medallion-print dress, then applied her makeup. After slipping into chic but comfortable sandals, Hallie gave the 900-square-foot loft she'd been renting one last look before heading out the door. To her relief, the taxi she'd called was already waiting outside the building. She placed her luggage inside the trunk. With a deep breath, she climbed into the car. Excitement bubbled up inside her—she was about to get that long-awaited stamp on her blank passport.

. . .

"How was your flight?" Her dad's voice echoed as if he were inside a tunnel.

"Long, but I'm finally sitting inside my London flat." Hallie took in the dimensions of the compact room, while the sort of smile one usually reserved for the promising start of a new relationship danced across her face.

"That's great. Your mom and I hope you find what you're searching for. Just remember we love you and where your home is."

"I know. Thank you for understanding why I need to do this. Call me tomorrow?"

"I will. Have fun."

Hallie disconnected. Fun was an understatement. To be here in person after planning the trip for so long in her mind was surreal. She inhaled the delightful aroma of the teashop attached to her flat. Though she was more of a latte fan, she'd soon sample the tea just to see if it tasted as good as it smelled.

The rooms were even tinier than she'd imagined. The square bathroom consisted of a pedestal sink, toilet, and shower barely big enough to maneuver inside. Standing in the center, with her arms outstretched, she could touch opposite walls of the room. Her kitchen contained only a small European mini-sized fridge, microwave, and a sink. She did have a compact washer and dryer in the hall closet, though. Would the walls start to close in on her?

Or would the elation of being here make up for her tiny living quarters? Only time would tell.

Hallie climbed the spiral metal staircase to the bedroom where her head almost touched the ceiling. The room, at full capacity, held a mattress on the tiled floor, a chair, and a corner closet. At least the room had a large window with a fabulous view of the narrow brick-paved street where a red double-decker bus rumbled below.

The lengthy to-do list popped into her mind. Her flat was close to the center of London yet hidden away from the busiest tourist spots. Her dear dad had helped her select the perfect place. Veering off the path most traveled was at the top of her agenda.

She slipped her toes into her shoes and headed downstairs. With a deep breath, she took in the historical brick buildings, the intricately carved light posts, and the colorful blooms of flowers in oversized pots. Statues seemed to be plentiful. Everyplace she looked, something stimulated her senses. People were out and about speaking with their delicious accents.

It wasn't long before she reached the River Thames. Glassy water rippled and reflected the sun. The magnificent city surrounding the grand river made her shiver with delight. Hallie gazed up at the London Eye—if she weren't afraid of heights, she'd go up in the gigantic observation wheel. The view would be breathtaking. Nothing could compare to actually experiencing the city in person. So much history surrounded her. Like the Grinch when he discovered the true meaning of Christmas, her heart swelled.

Across the river, Big Ben chimed. She stopped in her tracks—the rhythmic sound was almost hypnotic. Crap. It was happening again. The visions that she'd chalked up to an erotic dream on the plane. Unquestionable passion ignited deep inside her inner core. Heat rushed through her as the scent of leather and amber encompassed her. A vision of a man's lips caressing her body made her gasp with pleasure. She tried to focus on his blurred face, but it was unrecognizable, dreamlike. Hallie could feel his caresses as he all but devoured her on the walkway.

A pigeon flew down in front of her face. The bird's flapping wings broke the enchantment the clock held over her. She swallowed and glanced around to make sure no one had witnessed her odd behavior.

Still breathless and a bit confused at why she'd just hallucinated again, or whatever that was, she took a left on Reddington and was met with a half dozen cafés. Hallie wasn't hungry until she smelled the freshly brewed coffee and baking pastries. Her stomach growled in response to the heavenly aroma. It wouldn't hurt to grab a bite.

With so many choices, finding a place to eat wasn't as easy a task as it should have been. She settled on Lovely Café, not only because of the name but the sidewalk sign advertising fresh scones. Jetlag, culture shock, maybe even hunger—there had to be an explanation for what happened on the plane and at the clock.

Her face still flushed, she entered the restaurant, which resembled a cozy, eclectic living room. Hallie took a seat on a plush armchair next to the picture window. She let herself relax. An elderly couple lounged on a fuchsia loveseat on the far side of the room, sipping on tea in mismatched floral china, their legs touching. The burst of the passion she'd experienced hearing Big Ben flickered over her. She shook it off. The excitement of finally being in London probably had her senses in overdrive. Her eyes traveled around the charming room. Stacks of worn books were scattered throughout. She reached over to the round end table beside her and picked up a menu handwritten on a paper doily.

"Welcome to Lovely Café. What can I bring you?"

Hallie looked up from her charming menu at the young woman with straight-ironed brown hair. "An almond scone and a latte, please."

"Brilliant choice. Our almond scones are what keep people coming back."

Hallie smiled in return. She let herself relax further into the cushiony green chair.

The waitress placed a steaming latte and a scone on the table next to her chair. Hallie took a bite of the warm pastry, and it melted in her mouth. The latte didn't disappoint either. After she finished her snack, she made her way back out to the brick-paved sidewalk. As another pigeon flew by, the birthmark on her wrist tingled.

• • •

Graham McCoy tried to focus on the inventory in his shop and not on the fact that his ex had just taken away his sports car and his life savings. He raked his fingers through his hair. They'd tried to fix their relationship more than once but always fell short of any kind of real happiness. Barmy woman. He'd do good not to ever fall in love again.

At least she hadn't touched McCoy's Antiques, the store he'd inherited from his great-uncle seven years ago. At nineteen, he'd had nothing better to do, so he kept the place running. Now the shop would keep him on his feet, and he'd have a roof over his head, thanks to the attached flat. He could have moved back to the States, but his heart, what little of it was left, belonged in London.

Jane Whittaker, his full-time employee and somewhat of a mother hen, stepped in front of him and waved her hand. "You've been winding those pocket watches for an hour. Is something on your mind?"

Graham closed the gold watch in his hand, melancholy as ever. "I was just thinking about how lucky I am to be free from Abigail."

She primped the gray bun on top of her head. "Ah, well, you've been doing a lot of thinking lately. Maybe you need a break. I can finish this inventory. Why don't you take the rest of the day off? It's pleasant out now, but it's supposed to rain the rest of the week."

Graham placed the pocket watch back inside the glass case. "Sometimes I wonder who's really the boss here." He kissed her cheek. "Cheers then." He shut the door and took a deep breath.

Jane was right. He'd let Abigail and his sham of a marriage take residence in his brain far too long. They'd gotten along fine at first, and then it was as if their marriage were cursed. They started fighting about anything and everything. Even the sound of her voice had begun to irritate him. After trying to make it work for three years, they both called it quits. He could do nothing to please the woman. Until he gave her an uncontested divorce along with his prized car and savings. That had pleased her.

He snorted and continued to walk down the pavement to his favorite pub. Graham strolled into The Lion Den and ordered a pint of bitter. He took a swig and let the alcohol work its magic. More relaxed already, he glanced outside as a pretty brunette walked by. Her shoulder-length hair was shiny and bouncy, like she was the star of a shampoo commercial. He guessed she was an American on holiday from the wide-eyed way she was sightseeing. There was something familiar about her, though he couldn't place what. She had nice legs too.

He tossed down the rest of his drink and set outside to get a closer look. When he exited the pub, she was nowhere to be seen. Graham narrowed his eyes in the sunlight and looked every direction. She'd vanished. Oh well, it was probably for the best. Any woman who could capture and hold his attention like that had to be bad news. Pushing the brunette out of his mind, he made his way back to the pub.

• • •

Hallie tried to contain her excitement so she didn't squeal with delight like a child in a candy store inside the British Museum. The architecture of the building itself was amazing. The round reading room was fascinating—she'd never seen so many beautiful books—but it was the eighteenth-and nineteenth-century pieces in the Enlightenment gallery that made her heart go pitter-patter. Museums excited her … they enriched people's lives, the main reason Hallie had chosen to become a curator. Each ancient object was a reminder of how much had been experienced even before her lifetime and how much was sure to happen after. Tangible pieces of history helped her feel a part of something big and significant.

She left the building with a smile etched on her face. She loved the United States, but a little piece of her heart would always remain in London, if right inside that museum. She gave the building one last look before heading back to her flat. Her feet ached from walking too much. Deep in thought, she turned to hail a cab and inadvertently flung her arm right into someone's back. Her cheeks heated. "Excuse me."

"Bugger off."

Her mouth dropped open at his blatant rudeness. "I apologize, really."

He turned around to face her. Embarrassment and anger flooded through her as she met his blue—no, to be more precise, indigo—eyes. The man was tall, dark, and more than handsome. But his attitude was ugly.

The hard lines of his face softened. "Sorry, I'm pissed." His gaze traveled up and down her body. "It's you. You have nice ... legs."

She took a step back. He kept blinking as he stared, a sure sign he was trying to remember something; then he licked his lips as if she were covered in the finest London chocolate. His appreciation of her shouldn't have pleased her, but it did. The strong odor of alcohol radiated from his breath. "You're drunk."

"That's what I said, I'm pissed."

She gave him a look of disgust and turned away from him.

"Wait, don't go."

She kept walking.

"Fuck."

Hallie shook her head and hopped into the black cab, putting as much distance between them as she could.

Chapter 2

Light drizzle turned into a downpour. Hallie dashed under an awning to keep from getting soaked. Rain was to be expected in London, so when she'd woken up to sprinkles, she hadn't let it deter her from walking down the street. She'd have to purchase an umbrella if the weather continued at this intensity. With wet fingers, she pushed a wavy lock of hair behind her ear.

Two doors flanked the light gray building she was standing in front of. To her left, six glass panes were encased in the wooden door, and to her right, the door was solid with a number 9 displayed on top. McCoy's Antiques was etched in the glass of the large square window. It would be the perfect place to wait for the rain to ease up.

Hallie wiped her hands on her tight-fitting knit dress and stepped into the shop. The walls were painted off-white, with dark gray shelving and tables. The place was beautifully arranged and organized. Various crystal chandeliers hung from the ceiling, giving the place a sophisticated ambiance. She strolled over to an eighteenth-century stone vase that was priced at about 1,500 U.S. dollars. A little over her price range. The wall to her left held five French Louis Philippe mirrors. Beautiful but too expensive to have shipped home.

A woman with her gray hair held in a neat bun smiled at her. "Hello. Let me know if you need any assistance."

"Thank you. This place is beautiful."

"Cheers. The owner takes pride in making sure of that. Have a look around. We specialize in rare personal items."

Hallie walked over to a glass case filled with gold and silver pocket watches. She would have bought one for her dad, but he made her promise she wouldn't spend any of her budget on them. She was drawn to a large weathered bookcase filled with books dated all the way back to the fifteenth century. Her fingers traveled along the cracked spines. She pulled out a brown leather-bound book of poems written completely in French. The earthy vanilla scent of the old books was intoxicating. Hallie placed it back on the shelf and removed a Spanish book in its original, tattered vellum binding. Nice, but it wasn't what she was looking for. She rubbed her earlobe between her finger and thumb, taking in all the shop had to offer.

Her eyes landed on three journals resting on top of some stacked trunks. She bent over and picked up the books. Their matching red embossed leather bindings verified that they were a set. She opened the first one to discover the pages yellowed and frail, but the ink was legible. And they were written in English.

The journals were old, but she couldn't place the era. As if they had always belonged to her, with overwhelming protectiveness, she clutched them to her chest. There wasn't a price, but she'd pay whatever the cost. Nothing had ever called to her the way the journals had. What had come over her? A bit alarmed, she placed the books back down and stepped away. Her heart fell. She sensed that the journals were meant for her to find. She couldn't leave without them.

Hallie found the woman at the counter polishing a silver tray. "What is the price for these?"

The woman tilted her head. "Ah, those diaries have been around for a long time." She took the top one from Hallie and looked it over. "It's unmarked. I'll need to ask the owner."

Her teeth clamped down on her lower lip as she watched the woman disappear to the back. She waited at the counter and noticed an unusual pierced silver fruit bowl stunning enough to have belonged to royalty, and it probably had. What if the journals had as well? What if she couldn't afford them? She almost dropped the collected works when the drunken man she'd had a run-in with outside the museum stepped out of the back and moved toward her. If she weren't so determined to make the purchase, she'd turn around and find another antiques store without a bad-mannered ass running it.

"You're interested in my oldest set of diaries?"

Hallie opened her mouth to answer but had trouble forming the words. Did he not remember her? Her palms dampened. "Uh, yes. I'd like to purchase them."

"Odd thing about these is there aren't any dates written inside that I could see. Why would someone keep diaries without adding dates?"

Her face warmed. His toned body stretched the fabric of his shirt. The way he held himself was sexy as hell despite everything else about him. "I ... I don't know."

He placed the journal back on top of the ones she was holding. "Five thousand pounds for the lot."

Hallie did the math in her head and gasped. Her heart sank.

The man who did wicked things to her insides laughed. "I'm joking, of course."

She didn't find him amusing. Rather rude, actually. "Of course. They can't be worth more than nine hundred pounds. I mean, without dates, maybe less." Hallie tried to play it cool, hoping to get them to a price she could afford.

He put his hands in his pockets and stared into her eyes. "I'll let them go for one thousand pounds."

She held his gaze despite how uncomfortable he was making her. Something about him seemed so familiar, though she couldn't place why. The only time she'd met the guy had been briefly outside the museum. "In that case, I'll take them."

"One thing, the items I sell are very personal, so I like to get to know the customers who purchase them. I'm Graham McCoy." He held out his hand.

She paused, then placed her free hand in his. Raw, undeniable desire rushed through her body, making her light-headed.

She pushed the confusing feelings aside. "Hallie York from Washington, D.C. But we've already met."

"So you do recognize me."

With those unique, deep blue eyes and that face, not to mention his perfect body—of course she recognized him. "Well, you're not sloppy drunk today, but yes, I do."

"I'm sorry about that. You caught me at a bad time. I assure you I only get pissed every other day."

"Well, that's good then. That means you're only an ass half the time." She pursed her lips and paid him for her purchase.

Graham raised an eyebrow and handed her a receipt. "I couldn't help but notice the birthmark on your wrist."

Hallie glanced down at the dove-shaped spot. "Yes, it looks like a flying bird. I get that all the time."

He nodded as if he understood. "Staying in London long, then?"

"I'm leasing a flat down the street." She looked outside to the steady rain. "You don't have any umbrellas for sale, do you?"

He reached under the counter and handed her a black one. "Take mine. You can bring it back whenever you're finished with it."

She didn't want to owe this guy anything. "I wouldn't want to impose."

"I insist." He thrust the umbrella at her.

She hesitated, but the pounding of rain on the glass won out. "Fine. Thank you."

"Cheers."

• • •

Graham watched as his umbrella and Hallie York from Washington, D.C. took off down the pavement. He couldn't care less if he ever saw his umbrella again; Hallie was another matter. Not only was she gorgeous, but the almost identical birthmark they shared on opposite wrists also intrigued him.

He'd never actually read the diaries she purchased. Jane told him they had been around almost as long as the store and that she'd just moved them from inside a trunk yesterday. He was a sucker for American tourists, but the moment the books had left his sight, he'd regretted the hasty sale.

Maybe when she brought back his umbrella, he'd ask her if she'd had a look at them. He'd love to hear about what was written inside and maybe even get to know Hallie more. If he were smart though, he'd take back the umbrella and send her on her way. Curiosity killed the pussycat, as they said.

"Pretty woman," Jane interrupted his thoughts. She stood beside him polishing a wooden trinket box. He had no idea how long she'd been standing there or how long he'd been staring out the window.

"Really? I hadn't noticed."

She smiled. "Not all women are Abigail."

"I'm not sure it is worth the risk of finding out."

"Life without risks may be safe but not exciting. I haven't seen your eyes sparkle like that since the day you took over this store."

He chose to ignore her. "Did you get the new shipment in from the back?"

"Behind you."

Graham opened a rectangular box on the floor next to the counter. He removed the tissue paper from a vintage, off-white Victorian nightdress. An image of perky breasts with taut nipples underneath the thin cotton fabric flashed before his eyes. His hands slid over curvy hips and ran down a toned stomach to the treasure below. Desire tore through him. Then as quickly as the vision appeared, it vanished. He needed to get bonked or ease up on the bitter. Maybe both. He placed the nightie back into the box and handed it to Jane.

"Put this with the other clothing."

"You all right? You look a little flushed."

"I'm fine." On second thought, maybe a pint was just what he needed.

Chapter 3

Fresh from the shower, Hallie slipped on her silk robe. The smooth fabric glided over her skin. She stared into the mirror at the same old Hallie. She'd been a fool to think that the moment she arrived in London, somehow the void inside her would magically be filled. What if that never happened? What if she'd spent her whole life building up this trip and it turned out to be no more than an extended vacation? She ran a brush through her damp hair, and then padded barefoot into the kitchen to make herself a cup of the peach tea she'd gotten on the way home.

She took her mug of tea to into the living room. Even if London didn't change her somehow, she still had her career when she got back home to look forward to. Hallie curled her legs up and took a sip of the hot, spicy peach liquid.

She had a date planned with the antique journals beside her. She'd been eager to read them ever since her purchase that morning. After another sip of tea, she opened to the first entry, which was the detailed history of how Big Ben was built. She paused to brush her fingers over the paper. The indentations from the writer's pen zapped the tips of her fingers. The writing vanished before her eyes. Hallie glanced over at the cup of tea. Whoa, what was in that stuff? She blinked her eyes a few times and gazed down at the blank aged paper. From out of nowhere, confusion and deep sadness washed over her. Before she even realized that she was crying, a tear plopped down on the empty page. As the paper absorbed her teardrop, a different entry appeared. Hallie gasped.

My dearest Flora,

It's the little things, like the sweet scent of your hair, the way your eyes turn a deeper shade of brown when we become one, how you know me better than I know myself, that I will most miss when we depart. We've already experienced more passion than many ever have the privilege of, and for that I am grateful. But it is not enough. It will never be enough when it comes to you. My heart has and always will belong to you in this life or the next. I will find you, my love, have no misgivings.

Hallie struggled not to faint. She closed the journal and reopened it. The words she'd just read remained. There was no reasonable explanation other than that it didn't really happen. It had to be jetlag. She needed sleep. Tomorrow she'd be able to make sense out of what was really written inside the mysterious books. But against her better judgment, she turned to the next page.

My dearest Flora,

    Maybe the prophecy won't come to pass, but still, I can't bear to just let you go without a fight. There has to be a way we can prepare ourselves for what may come. I've contacted a powerful seer. He thinks there may be a way. We must hurry, since we were not given a definite time of our departure. Even if my heart is ripped out of my chest, it will still beat for you.

Hallie wiped her eyes. Pain tore through her as she clutched the journal. As much as she was compelled to keep reading about undying love, she needed to sleep. Something was happening to her, and she was almost certain it wasn't healthy. She placed the journal back on top of the others. With a deep sigh and unexplainable longing, she made her way upstairs, but not before her cell phone alerted her to a call.

"Mom?"

"Hi, honey, are you enjoying London so far?"

"Yes." She sniffled. "It's good to hear your voice."

"Have you been crying?"

She cleared her throat. "No, I probably just picked up a little cold."

"Are you getting enough to eat?"

"Yes. The food is amazing."

"Is England everything you thought it would be?"

It wasn't. In fact, she was more alone and confused than ever. Hallie wanted to confide in her mom, but didn't want her worrying about her any more than she already did. "Yes."

Her mom paused. "Good. That's good."

The silence grew awkward. "How's Dad?"

"He's great. A bit worried about you traveling abroad alone."

"I'm not a little girl anymore."

"Tell that to your dad."

"Mom, do you believe in supernatural occurrences?"

"What kind of silly question is that? Are you okay?"

Hallie sighed. "I'm fine. Just tired. I should head to bed. Love you guys."

• • •

"Cheers," Graham said as Jane left the store. The woman was a godsend. Much because of her help, business was thriving. He whistled as he strolled over to lock the door. Just as he turned to head to his flat, loud knocks on the door stopped him short. People really should learn to pay attention to closed signs.

A smile registered on his face when he realized his interruption wasn't an illiterate customer, but Hallie York standing outside his shop. She smiled back at him and held up his umbrella.

Her sexy smirk was hard to ignore, so he opened the door. "Come in."

She stepped inside, dressed in form-fitting khakis and a red pleated halter top. The woman was elegant and probably out of his league. "Thanks for letting me borrow this."

Graham took the umbrella from her outstretched hand. Her bare shoulders begged to be kissed. Instead, he shook her hand. "Cheers."

Her eyes widened. "I, uh, need to talk to you about the journals I purchased."

He let go of her soft, manicured hand. "Sorry, no refunds."

"No, I don't want to return them." She looked around. "Do you know where they came from?"

"That is confidential, and I didn't acquire them. My uncle, the previous owner did."

She frowned. "Oh. Do you have time to talk? There's something about ... I just ..." She clasped her hands in front of her and looked away.

Maybe she was trying to ask him out on a date. Her soulful brown eyes gazed into his. He could go on a few fun dates without getting serious. "I was on my way out to the pub. Would you care to join me?"

Hallie hesitated. "Sure, that'd be great."

He locked up, and they made their way down to The Lion Den. She was fidgety—nothing like the confident woman the other day. "So, what did you want to talk about? I never got a chance to actually read the diaries. I'm curious. Did you find any dates?"

She pursed her red lips. "Maybe it's best if I got a drink before we discuss them."

They entered his favorite pub and walked across the dark hardwood floors to the gold rounded bar. Graham watched Hallie's face to see if she appreciated the atmosphere of the place as much as he did. She glanced around the rich burgundy-colored walls, up to the original tin ceiling, and her eyes sparkled. He couldn't hide his satisfied grin. "What would you like?"

Hallie rubbed her earlobe. "Any white wine. Thanks."

Graham nodded at the barman. He ordered a bitter and a pricey glass of wine. After he paid for their drinks, they carried their glasses to a private round table in the corner. They sipped on their drinks in awkward silence.

Hallie fidgeted in her seat. "I really don't know how to say this, so I thought it best to show you."

He was more than a little curious at her reluctance, so he turned to the first page. The problem was the page was blank. The woman had to be messing with him. Maybe to get him back for the way he treated her outside the museum. "Is this some kind of joke?"

"No, I wish it were." She took his hand. "Try running your fingers along the paper."

Her insistent gaze persuaded him to do as she instructed. His fingertips touched the page. His heart almost stopped when handwritten words appeared. Hallie nodded her head and coaxed him to read. His mouth went dry. He took a long pull from his bitter before going any farther.

My dearest Edmund,

Your smile, your eyes, the way just your touch can make the world right after a dreadful day. I cannot comprehend leaving you. Not falling asleep wrapped in your strong arms is unbearable. Not tasting or feeling how much you love me is excruciating. You're the reason I breathe now and always. Someday, I may not recognize your body, but our hearts and souls are connected. We'll find a way back to each other, my love.

Graham closed the diary and laughed. "Nice party trick with the disappearing ink. What kind of fool do you play me for?"

Hallie sat up tall. "This is not a trick. This is ... well, I don't know what this is. But at least now I know I'm not crazy. You saw it too."

He raked his fingers through his hair and tossed back the rest of his drink. "I saw something. Just not sure what."

"Look, I don't exactly know either, but it seems we were meant to read these diaries together. When I read the passages, they are addressed to Flora, and when you read them, they are addressed to Edmund."

He tried to grasp what she was attempting to convince him of. "I skimmed over these the day you purchased them. I don't recall the names Flora or Edmund. Or this undying love mumbo jumbo."

With a curt nod and a tilt of her head, she replied, "I think I unlocked the passages."

"And how the bloody hell did you do that?"

She avoided his eyes. "I cried on the page," she mumbled.

"You *cried* on it?" He raised his voice louder than intended. As pretty as she was, she was just as barmy as his ex.

"It's hard to explain. I felt this compelling sadness, and before I knew what was happening, a tear slipped off my face and plopped onto the blank page, revealing the first hidden entry."

He didn't need this. He didn't need her or her brilliant body. He was an idiot to let her affect him after what he'd just been through with Abigail. "I think it's a good idea if you take the diary and go."

She placed her soft hand over his. A familiarity that he hadn't felt when they'd touched before took him by surprise. "Please. Just read the next entry. I read two. That was all I could see. Maybe if you read two, I'll be able to read another."

The pleading in her eyes caught him off guard. Graham shook his head but turned the page.

My dearest Edmund,

    And my heart for you. The seer will help us prepare. I am afraid, but will not give up hope.

Graham crossed his arms and leaned back in his chair. "You expect me to believe this is, what? Some kind of magical book?"

"I know this sounds crazy." She paused to take a sip of her wine. "But I think Flora and Edmund are ghosts trying to communicate with us to help them."

"To help them what?"

"Find each other ... in the afterlife."

Graham rubbed his eyes. Despair filled him. Not because of the diary, but because he couldn't seem to find a woman in her right mind. "Ms. York. It's been a long day. I should get home."

She pursed her lips and grabbed the book from the table. "I guess we're through then."

He watched her hair bounce as she stormed out of the pub without a backward glance. Un-fucking-believable. Without hesitation, he chugged down the rest of his drink.

Chapter 4

Hallie rushed past dozens of people milling around outside the pub. She should have known that infuriating man wouldn't believe her. She had a hard time believing it herself. Magic books and seers. Crazy, right? It took her two days to come up with the ghost theory. It fit. Not that she'd ever accepted ghosts were real before, let alone could communicate with the living, but it had to be something along those lines. She'd shown the journal to four random people, and they saw only the original written words. For some reason, these two souls had chosen her and Graham McCoy to help them.

There was no one else she could talk to about this. Graham was it. They were in this together, whether they liked it or not. Maybe this phenomenon, rather than the idea London could be her birthplace, was the purpose for her being here. She could choose to ignore what was happening or be a part of something extraordinary.

Deep inside every curator was a desire to believe there was a remote chance he or she had come across an antiquity that captured the very essence of the people or culture to which it once belonged. The set of journals were a once-in-a-lifetime acquisition. She wasn't about to ignore something so special.

• • •

Graham unwrapped the gold-mounted Bohemian glass perfume bottle and placed it on the tabletop next to a pearl picture frame. Hallie had preoccupied his thoughts for most of the day. He couldn't explain what had happened last night. It had to be some sort of hoax. The woman was playing him. If those diaries did have some kind of magic, why was it Hallie and not he who had discovered it? Why not his uncle? There was no way those diaries contained magic, let alone ghosts' correspondence. No, she was after something. Women always were.

"That's lovely." Jane pointed to the perfume bottle.

Well, younger women, anyway. His employee was about as pure-hearted as they came. "I purchased it last week, and it just arrived."

"You take after your uncle. He always found the hidden gems."

"Speaking of hidden gems, the set of diaries we sold to Ms. York—is there a way to find out where Louis acquired them?" If there was a mystery to be solved, he'd get to the bottom of it.

Jane paused for a moment. "Mr. McCoy used to keep his records in the basement. They may still be down there."

He frowned. The place was an unorganized mess when he came along seven years ago. "I looked through all his old stuff when I took over. I don't remember seeing anything."

"I imagine if you keep looking, you'll find them. Doubtful that he took them with him."

She had a valid point. People didn't take their work with them to the grave. His uncle was unmarried, unengaged, and a bit of a loner. The records were sure to still be around somewhere. "Cheers, Jane. I'll be downstairs."

Graham turned on the light and made his way down the steep steps. At least the cobwebs were no longer a part of the decor thanks to his thorough cleaning. He paused to look around. The back wall lined with shelves had already been organized; the opposite wall held boxes that he'd already gone through. His eyes landed on the dark-stained oak armoire to his right. The thing was too heavy and large to get up the stairs. Fuck if he knew how it ever got down here in the first place.

As he recalled, it contained some personal items he'd felt awkward rummaging through in the past since he'd barely known his uncle. He opened the middle door. An earthy wooden smell filled the air. Outdated pressed clothing hung on hangers. Two pairs of loafers sat in the bottom. He moved the clothes aside to reveal the back of the cabinet and nothing else. Not surprised, he closed the door and tried the one to his left. His uncle's broken glass collection. The man sold invaluable antiques and saved worthless chunks of white glass. He scratched the back of his head. As useless as the shards were, he didn't feel right tossing out the old man's keepsakes after he'd generously given him his shop. Graham closed the door.

He tried the last cabinet. Just as he remembered—more rubbish. Memorabilia that meant nothing to Graham ... antique shaver, empty soda bottle, ticket stubs to theater shows, and a photo box filled with photographs. Graham reached for the door but hesitated. He grabbed the box and removed the lid. He took out the stack of photos. The old photographs weren't of people as he'd originally thought—they were the items he'd acquired for the shop. Graham flipped through the pictures and recognized a few of the objects he'd sold the first year he'd taken over.

The diaries. The box fell from his hands, causing the photos to scatter all over the concrete floor. He turned over the picture. Handwritten on the back was the name Harriet Brown, January 11, 2000. Graham tucked the photo inside his shirt pocket. His heart raced as fast as his feet up the stairs.

"You found something?"

He hugged Jane. "That I did. I need to run an errand. You can lock up for me?"

"Of course."

Graham stepped out into the drizzling rain and got into his dark blue sedan. He pulled out his smartphone and looked up Harriet Brown. Could the woman who owned a bed-and-breakfast in the countryside be the same Harriet he was looking for? Only one way to be sure. He punched the address into his GPS.

Fifty minutes later, Graham pulled into a long, winding drive that led up to the large, very square, red brick house. Surrounded by beautiful countryside, the location was ideal for a bed-and-breakfast. He parked his car in the only one of the eight spots available. The wooden sign over the door announced he'd arrived at Brown's B and B.

When he stepped up to the door, a woman in her late fifties carrying a basket of freshly picked herbs came around from the side garden. "Cheers. Are you looking for a place to stay?"

Graham cleared his throat. "I'm looking for Harriet Brown."

"You've found her. I'm Harriet."

He removed the photo from his pocket and handed it to her. "Did you sell these to my uncle, Louis McCoy?"

An odd look danced over her face. "Yes."

"Can you tell me more? A customer of mine purchased the diaries, and she'd like a better history of them."

"Those were from my husband's great-grandmother's estate." She paused. "I'd love to help you, but I need to prepare dinner. I mostly run this place by myself."

"I promise not to take much of your time."

She tilted her head. "If you want to come back tomorrow, I may have more time to chat."

"Do you have any vacancies? I could use a break from the city anyway." He tried his best to hide the sarcasm from his voice. He didn't really want to frolic in the country, but he needed answers.

"I may have one. If you follow me inside, I'll check."

Graham held the door open for her. They entered the foyer, and she went behind a desk. She sat down her basket and flipped through a tattered book.

"If you need the room for only one night, I have an opening."

The historical room papered in a floral design wasn't his cup of tea, but he needed to prove that Hallie York was insane. Maybe then he could get the woman off of his mind and get back to being a carefree bachelor. "I'll take it."

She swiped his credit card and handed it back to him. "Right upstairs, third room on your left. Dinner's in an hour and the dining room is behind me."

"Looking forward to it." Graham nodded and headed upstairs. The floorboards creaked a bit under his feet. He opened the door to his accommodations. The small room was papered in green velvet. The full-sized bed looked comfy enough topped with a cream bedspread. He wouldn't need to use the dark wooden dresser, since he'd arrived with only the clothes on his back. He walked over to the window, which overlooked a duck pond. Charming.

With a sigh, he sat down on the bed. How the bloody hell had he let yet another woman turn his life upside down?

Chapter 5

Emptiness settled deep within her chest. Relentless tears rolled down Hallie's face as she continued to read, the taste of salt in her mouth.

> I hold on to each precious moment I have left with you. Each day is a gift, and I open it with great anticipation and joy. You've already given me so much, but I am greedy and I want more.

Her breath caught in her throat as she closed the journal. She now knew why there were no dates written on the pages—time was irrelevant to the people who'd penned the entries. She let out a deep sigh. What was happening to her was unreal. She had to help the ghosts find one another. A love like that shouldn't die—even in death.

The scary thing was, the more she read about Flora and Edmund, the more her life seemed inadequate. Sure she had a family, a degree, her career, but what about love? It wasn't as if she'd never had a relationship, but the men had never held her interest for long. She suddenly desired more. Unyielding passion like the ghosts shared. She sighed. Maybe a love so strong was dangerous. Her throat burned from the emotion she held down.

What was wrong with her? Maybe once she took care of putting the spirits to rest, she'd be able to relax and enjoy the rest of her stay in London. She wiped her eyes and grabbed her purse and keys. With her mind occupied, the walk to McCoy's Antiques was a quick one. Before she knew it, she was reaching for the door.

She stepped up to the woman whom she recognized from the other day. "Hello, I'm looking for Graham."

"He's taken the day off, Ms. York."

She was taken aback that the lady knew her name. "Do you know where I could reach him? It's important."

"He stayed at Brown's B and B last night. If you hurry, he may still be there. I think he'd be pleased to see you." She winked before walking away.

Graham didn't seem like the bed-and-breakfast type. And she highly doubted he'd be happy to see her. But she wasn't going to let that stop her. Plan in motion, she took out her phone to call a cab.

• • •

After eating what had to be the biggest brunch ever, Graham pushed in his chair and set out to find the chef. He spotted Mrs. Brown washing down the speckled countertops. If he wasn't mistaken, the woman had been avoiding him. "That was delicious, and the room was comfortable last night ..."

She smiled. "You slept well?"

He had, despite that fact he'd had vivid dreams of the faceless woman in the nightdress. The way her body had moved under his was so real. He was aroused just thinking about it. "Yes. But I really should get going. Could you please spare a moment to tell me about the diaries now?"

Mrs. Brown placed the washcloth into the sink and wiped her hands on her apron. "I'm glad you enjoyed your accommodations. Let's take a glass of tea out to the courtyard."

Graham rubbed the back of his head. "Tea sounds brilliant." He had to keep himself from tapping his foot while she took her time preparing the cold drinks. If he didn't know any better, he'd think she was stalling for some reason.

He followed her outside. Once they sat down on a stone bench in front of the small fishpond, he tried again. "So, the diaries, they were your husband's great-grandmother's?"

She took a sip of her herbal tea. "Yes. When she passed, my husband handled her estate. Then when he passed, I had to sell a lot of our belongings to keep this place up and running. It's more expensive than you think to run a bed-and-breakfast."

"I'm terribly sorry for your losses."

"Thank you."

He waited for her to go on, but she didn't. "I assure you that the items you sold to McCoy's were well taken care of. Did you ever notice anything unusual about the diaries?"

"Unusual?" She almost choked on her drink. "How do you mean?"

"Never mind. Just, did your husband's great-grandmother's name happen to be Flora?"

She hesitated. "No, it was Catherine."

He wasn't getting anywhere. "Was Catherine married?"

"Yes. Several times." She paused. "Though the diaries did belong to Catherine, they were not hers personally. She was an antiques collector. I believe she picked them up along with a lot of her other possessions over the years. I can't be sure where she got them, but she liked to go to the antiques fairs in Chelsea."

"Brilliant. I'll try there." He took a long drink of his beverage. "Thank you for the drink and the information. I really ..."

"Graham?"

The sound of Hallie York's voice around the corner of the house made his heart skip a beat.

He stood up. "What are you doing here?" The woman looked good enough to eat dressed in tight white jeans and an off-the-shoulder plum-colored top. She had no right to look that good around him. Whatever game she was playing, she wasn't playing fair.

She moved her sunglasses to the top of her head and peered at him with those inviting eyes. "I was about to ask you the same question."

Harriet cleared her throat.

Graham turned to her. "This is a lovely establishment. I'll be sure to recommend it." Before the woman could respond, he grabbed Hallie's wrist and dragged her away from the B and B owner.

"Let go of me!"

He dropped his hand. "What are you after?"

"I am after whatever is happening with those journals."

"Nothing is happening. Why don't you take your purchase and head back to the United States where you belong?"

Her mouth fell open. "You're so rude. Believe me, if I didn't need you to be able to read the entries, I'd never speak to you again."

He raked his fingers through his hair. "I don't need this."

"Is that why you came here? To get away from me?"

"Don't flatter yourself. I needed some rest and relaxation. Period."

"Who was she?" She plopped her sunglasses back over her eyes.

"Who was who?"

"The woman who made you such an asshole."

Graham couldn't hold in the laugh that she'd triggered. "That would be my ex-wife."

"I'm not enemy number one. I'm not crazy or trying to trick you. I'm a curator for the Smithsonian National Museum of Natural History, and I know something special when I see it."

His chest tightened. "You really believe this is something supernatural?"

"Without a doubt. Now are you going to help me help Flora and Edmund, whoever or whatever they are?"

"Do I have a choice?" He'd play along until he figured out what the woman was after and why.

"There's always a choice." She removed one of the diaries from her purse. "Do you want to see the next entry?"

He cringed but opened the book.

My dearest Edmund,

Our passion only grows stronger with each breath we take. Even though the seer believes that everything we've tried to connect us will get jumbled in the afterlife, I have faith that our love will find a way.

Graham closed the diary and handed it back to Hallie, his heart full of sentiments he couldn't express. This was like being pissed without getting to enjoy the taste or the buzz. He shook it off. "True love has always fallen short for me, no matter how close I thought I was to having it. What these two people shared was rare." No woman was going to make a fool out of him again. He would prove this was all a hoax and stick it to the woman who was trying to trick him. "I was just on my way to Chelsea. Care to join me?"

She certainly didn't try to hide the satisfied smile on her face. "I have nowhere else I have to be."

Chapter 6

Graham's hands gripped the steering wheel as he stared straight ahead. He hadn't explained why he was going to Chelsea, and she hadn't asked. For all she knew, that was where the closest loony bin was located and he taking her on a one-way trip.

She might as well make the most of the journey and sightsee from the window. Lush green land rolled on for miles under the bluish-gray sky.

He turned up the air in his car and pushed up his sleeves.

She let out a gasp at the bird-shaped mark on his wrist. "Your birthmark. It's just like mine!"

He glanced over at her wrist. "It's similar."

"Why didn't you tell me?"

He shrugged and kept his focus on the road ahead.

She couldn't take her eyes off his birthmark. "Don't you find it curious? We were chosen, Graham McCoy, maybe even before we were born. There's not a doubt in my mind about that now."

"Don't get your knickers in a bunch. Lots of people have birthmarks on their wrists."

She raised an eyebrow. "Shaped like flying doves?"

"Sure, why not? Seen the whole world, have you?"

He could deny what was happening all he wanted. It didn't change anything. She took a deep breath and chose her words carefully. "This is all new to me, too. I haven't made a habit of believing in unnatural beings." She paused. "But I think for this to work, you're going to have to keep an open mind."

"I'm trying. The diaries belonged to the bed-and-breakfast owner, or rather, her husband's great-grandmother. It appears she may have picked them up from an antiques fair in Chelsea."

"So that's why we're going there."

"Yes."

Hallie took in the view as they drove by many eighteenth-century homes. The old village atmosphere drew her right in. The place was abundant with people, art galleries, and antiques shops. Graham made a rude gesture to the double-decker bus that cut them off before pulling onto a side road to park.

He walked around as she was getting out of the car. "We'll try Town Hall first. A lot of antiques fairs are held there."

Hallie only nodded as she took in the activity around them. She'd never seen so many bicycles lined up on sidewalks. Or happy people. The aromas from all the cafés made her stomach growl with hunger. She shouldn't have skipped lunch. She'd planned on eating at the bed-and-breakfast but had completely forgotten when she'd come into contact with Graham. She ignored her appetite and followed him through the busy sidewalks.

"Why do you think Flora and Edmund chose us to help them?"

"I'm not convinced that they have. But if so, maybe they will realize they've made a terrible mistake and pick someone else." He laughed. "I've not exactly been successful in the romance department."

"This is not a joke."

"So you keep saying."

She wasn't convinced Flora and Edmund had made the right decision either. If the two of them couldn't even get along, there was little chance they'd be of much help.

"Enough about me. How about you? What's your guess?"

"I have no idea." Maybe she'd tell him about how she'd always felt connected and drawn to London, but not right now. And if she told him about what she'd seen when she heard Big Ben, he'd think her even more insane. Her stomach growled again, this time loud enough for him to hear.

"Are you hungry?"

No sense in denying it. "I haven't eaten since seven."

He turned around in the opposite direction. "Let's get you fed then. We have a lot of ground to cover, and I don't think you will be able to do it on an empty stomach."

She didn't argue. They slipped into the nearest café. The waitress must have thought them a couple since she sat them at a private table with a vase of fresh flowers. What would it be like to be on an actual date with Graham? She pushed that thought out of her mind as fast as it had entered it.

. . .

Graham watched Hallie devour her sandwich. The woman must have been starving. He took a drink of his water in awe of her appetite. She lifted another bite to her mouth, revealing the dove mark on her wrist. Was there something to their shared birthmark? If so, what did it mean? There were so many questions running through his mind. She was unlike any woman he'd ever dated. Not that he was dating her. Bloody hell, what was she doing to him? He was supposed to be playing her. He was not about to be the one getting played. Not this time.

"So how long have you worked for the Smithsonian?"

She wiped her mouth on a napkin. "I got the job right before I planned this trip. I don't officially start until I get back to the States."

"Fresh out of university then?" He leaned back in his chair. "You're just a baby."

"Yes, but hardly a baby. I'm twenty-three. How about you?"

"Twenty-six."

"Good to know, but I meant college."

Ah, a time when he was restless and unsure of his future. "I took some classes here and there. Once I moved here and took over my great-uncle's shop, I quit going."

"Moved here, as in London?"

At the moment, their conversation flowed easily as if they were old friends. Yet he doubted Hallie York would ever be his friend. "I'm originally from Rhode Island."

"You were an East Coaster like me. I thought your accent was a bit off."

He laughed. Maybe he wasn't as British as he thought he'd become. "Really? I've lived in London for seven years, though it seems like forever."

"Would you ever move back?"

He watched her finger trace the edge of her sweaty glass. The movement was simple yet somewhat sensual. "No. I belong here."

"Do you have family in Rhode Island?"

"A sister. She comes for a visit every few years."

"That's nice, but it must be hard."

"It's easier than you think. With technology, we're able to keep in touch even more so than we did when we lived in the same country. How about you?"

She smiled and stood up. "I have my parents. We're close. We should get going."

He followed her out of the café onto the busy street. Town Hall held many vendors selling their goods. He showed the picture of the diaries around without any luck. Hallie stayed by his side. If they weren't on a quest, this would almost seem like a date.

One person after another shook his or her head and denied ever seeing the diaries. When they'd hit every antiques dealer inside, he stood baffled.

"What about the seer? How do you think one goes about finding someone like that?"

He shoved his hands in his pocket. "You can't be serious."

"It can't hurt."

"Well, it's not as if we can just ring one up."

"Maybe we can. It's a start. I'm sure we'll get some fraudulent fortune tellers, but we have no other leads."

That was what he feared. There seemed to be enough fraud in his life.

Chapter 7

Hallie pressed her lips together as she sat in front of Madame Epiphany. The woman with a wild mass of toffee-colored curls gazed into her crystal ball and chanted in some indistinguishable language. Her black painted fingernails had little half-moons applied on them. It was everything Hallie could do to keep a straight face. Graham glanced over at her with a wide smirk. Feeling foolish, she avoided his eyes and focused on Madame Epiphany. Maybe this was a bad idea after all.

The woman's unnaturally blue eyes, probably from the help of colored contacts, widened as what could only be described as absolute alarm flashed over her face. She paused for what seemed like an eternity. "I feel the power of the spirits with you two stronger than I ever have with anyone."

Her words held Hallie's attention. "What do you see?"

Madame Epiphany perused the globe of quartz crystal. She frowned and handed them back their money. "I'm afraid I've seen all I can. Live your life like there is no tomorrow."

Graham grabbed the cash and stood up. "Let's go. This is rubbish. Just like I knew it would be."

Hallie ignored him and watched the woman back away from them. "Wait. What did you see?"

Madame Epiphany shook her head.

Hallie slapped her hands on the table. "Tell me!"

"Pain. Excruciating pain." Her voice was barely more than a whisper.

Hallie shuddered and swallowed the lump in her throat. Graham grabbed her trembling hand. He pulled her out of the door before she knew what was happening.

"Don't let her scare you." He dropped her hand. "We knew going in this was probably not going to get us anywhere."

"There was something about her face. Phony or not, this time she really saw *something*."

"She's just a good actress. Don't buy into it."

Uneasiness settled in the pit of her stomach. "But she gave us our money back. How do you explain that?"

"I don't know. It could all be a part of her plan to suck us in. Maybe next time, she charges us more since she is so afraid of what she sees. Before we know it, we are giving her our life savings to tell us everything. It happens. I'm just not that easy to fool."

He had a point. There was no sense in arguing about it even if she was worried Madame Epiphany really did see something less than desirable in store for them. "Neither am I. Maybe you're right."

"Of course I am."

Twilight fell upon them, and they had a long drive ahead. Spending any time with Graham alone at night wouldn't be a good idea. Her attraction to him was growing. "It's getting late. We can start fresh tomorrow."

"I do have a shop to run."

He couldn't possibly be thinking of carrying on with everyday life as if none of this had ever happened. "Don't you get a vacation?"

He sighed. "I guess I can ask Jane if she wants to pick up some extra hours until we can get this sorted out."

"Thank you. I could even help you out if needed."

"You?"

"Sure, why not?"

"Thanks, but that won't be necessary. Jane can handle it."

Triumphant, she followed Graham to his car. A dazzling star shot across the darkened sky, sending chills over her neck and shoulders. Her first witness of an actual shooting star at that very moment could be a mere coincidence. Though she doubted it.

• • •

After waking Hallie, Graham dropped her off. She'd slept most of the way home. He obviously didn't get that luxury, and he had way too much time to puzzle over things. Unsettled, he headed to his own flat. Even though he'd sworn Madame Epiphany's vision was rubbish, she'd scared the bloody hell out of him. He'd never really believed in ghosts or magic before, but now he was having second thoughts. If such things did exist, he'd rather be oblivious. It was too late—Hallie wouldn't let this go until she was at the heart of whatever was happening. And what was with her offering to help him at the store? Was she being generous, or did she have some other hidden agenda?

Graham climbed into bed. The moment his head touched the pillow, the vision of the woman in the Victorian nightdress recurred even stronger this time. His hands reached under the thin fabric of her gown and traveled the length of her exquisite body. She lifted the article of clothing over her head. He cupped her breasts and brought one to his mouth to taste her sweet and slightly salty skin. She reached for him. He tried to see her face, but it was a blur.

Fantasy or not, he gave in and let her take hold of him. Her soft hands stroked and squeezed him, bringing him to the edge of insanity. He buried his face in her neck and savored her candy scent. Unable to control the buildup any longer, he thrust into her slick haven. She threw her head back and moaned, bringing them both to immediate release. Sweat beaded over his body. Graham opened his eyes to find himself alone.

He sprung out of bed and headed to his shop, not bothering with getting dressed. Naked, he turned on one of the overhead chandeliers and rushed to the open chest of drawers that held what he sought. Graham picked up the nightie and hugged it to his heaving chest. He smelled her on the cotton. Her sweet scent that had driven him mad. His heart ached as if he'd lost his best friend. Bloody hell, he was in love with a ghost.

He looked up to the ceiling. "Flora? Are you there?" He paused. "Anyone?"

Nothing happened. The only sound was his own breathing. Was he losing his mind? He kept hold of the nightdress and turned off the light. The best sex he'd had in his life and it wasn't even real. He crawled back into bed with the vintage gown. Wishing and waiting for the woman whose face he couldn't see but whose body he had memorized to return to him, if only for a moment, to prove he hadn't imagined the whole thing.

• • •

Hallie woke with a start. She tried to fill her deprived lungs with oxygen, but her gasps for air frightened her. Death had been close. Before she sat up in bed and opened her eyes, she'd thought it had come. She ran her hands over her dampened arms and shuddered. It was just a nightmare. It had seemed so real. But it couldn't have been—she was alive and alone in her bed. After a deep breath, as deep as she could while petrified, she concentrated only on her heartbeat.

She moved her wet hair away from her face. Wishing she had something stronger than coffee or tea in the flat, Hallie pushed herself to get up from bed. It was too early to get up, but she'd never be able to go back to sleep with her body soaked in perspiration.

Madame Epiphany had gotten to her. Hallie had to keep her cool or Graham wouldn't help her any further. If only she knew what Flora and Edmund needed them to do.

If nothing else, a quick shower might help her relax. Hallie stepped into the tiny stall. With a hard turn of her wrist, hot water sluiced down her back. She breathed in the steam and lowered her shoulders. Finally loosened up, she stood under the showerhead so the stream could rain over her face.

Arousal came out of nowhere. His lips traveled along her collarbone. She wrapped her legs around his hard, wet body. The striking scent of leather and amber enveloped her. The only other time she'd smelled this scent was in front of Big Ben. It wasn't real, but she let herself revel in the vision.

She wanted to see his face, but it wouldn't come into focus. Her brain screamed for her to get answers, but her body demanded her brain to shut the hell up. Her body won out as she let him devour her. It was cold water that finally shocked her out of her trance. Hallie grabbed the handle and shut off the icy flow. Her only concept of time was that she'd been lost in blissful ignorance as long as it took for the hot water to run out.

• • •

The sound of pounding on the downstairs door made Hallie gasp. She sat up from her bed still in her robe. Remembering she'd gone back to sleep with wet hair, she grabbed a ponytail holder to tame her inevitable bedhead. Barefoot, she padded down the stairs. She pulled her robe tighter around her before peeking out the cracked door. Graham stood there, confident, holding two paper cups and a small white bag. Unlike her, he looked fresh and wide awake. The yellow button-up shirt paired with blue jeans was enough to make her mentally fan herself. Though everything he'd worn so far had done the same. There was just something about a well-dressed man, especially one with a British accent.

She opened the door wider. "I wasn't expecting you so soon."

"I couldn't sleep. I brought caffeine. Wasn't sure if you'd want coffee or a latte, so I got one of each."

"Latte's great. Just let me get dressed. You can have a seat." She motioned to the sofa in front of them.

After he sat down, she rushed upstairs to her room. She shut the door and hurried to find something to wear. Pulling open drawers, she fumbled through clothing. Her heart raced. She decided on her favorite medallion-print dress and sandals. A quick look in the mirror revealed her hair wasn't as bad as she'd thought. She brushed through her locks and ran some tinted lip balm over her lips. A few swipes of dark eyeliner and she was ready.

When she entered the room, Graham whistled. Heat rose to her cheeks. A man had never actually whistled at her before. Flirted sure, but whistling was for movies.

"You look great. If you want me to concentrate on ghost hunting, maybe you should wear something less flattering next time."

"You're impossible."

He laughed. "I've been told that more than once."

"I bet you have." She took the latte from him. "Thanks."

He took a croissant out of the sack and gave it to her.

She tore the fresh bread apart and took a bite. Carbs happened to be just what she needed. "Were you able to get the day off?"

"Two weeks actually. Jane seemed thrilled I was taking some time off. I never really have except for a few sick days here and there."

She reached over to the table and brought the journals over to them. "We should read as much as we can. The answers we're looking for could be inside." He moved closer to her until their legs almost touched. God help her, she wanted them to. Maybe she'd act on her feelings once they helped Flora and Edmund reunite.

"Then what are we waiting for?"

After a drink of his coffee, Graham opened to the first page. "Let's reread it from the beginning so as to not miss anything."

Pushing away the desire to slide over two inches closer, she nodded and began to read, "My dearest Flora ..."

Chapter 8

Graham watched Hallie's full lips move as she read. He struggled to hear the words, as the overwhelming desire to kiss her grew stronger by the minute. He wanted to tell her about the sexual fantasies he'd been having about Flora, or at least he thought it was Flora. But there was a good chance she'd laugh at him or think him some kind of pervert. It had been far too long since he'd made love to a woman. He hardly thought sexual encounters with a ghost counted.

When he wasn't looking at Hallie's lips, his eyes took in her long, bare legs. The woman was wicked wearing a dress around him. It would be all too easy to lift up the fabric and pull her on top of his lap. He would bet her panties had some sort of lace on them. Maybe she was wearing a thong. Visions of her bare ass caused his zipper area to tighten.

"Are you even listening?"

He swallowed down his desire and focused on what she was saying. "Yes. Sorry, can you read that last bit again?" He'd set out to prove the woman was crazy. Truth was, he was the one losing his mind.

"If all else fails, I'll know you by your scent. The finest sweet confection with the hint of earthy salt."

His heart raced. Flora's scent. Sweet and salty. It was her. He was having sex with a ghost. Bloody hell.

"You're pale. Are you okay?"

He stood up and paced. When that didn't help, he unbuttoned the top three buttons of his shirt. "I'm fine. It's hot in here ... I need some air."

Graham exited Hallie's flat without another word. None of what was happening made any sense. If Flora was so in love with

Edmund, why was she coming to him for sex? And on top of that, he couldn't deny the fact that he was strongly attracted to Hallie. Until he understood what was going on, he'd keep Flora's mysterious visits to himself. He stepped out into the drizzling rain and filled his lungs with the damp air. His world was crumbling around him. Everything he once thought to be true and real was corrupt. Ever since his divorce, it was as though he'd never have a solid foundation under him again. There had only been one constant all his life. He took out his phone and called his sister.

"Is it a bad time?"

"I always have time for you, little brother. How are you?" Gretchen's rising tone indicated she knew something was wrong.

"I'm fucking brilliant."

"Still trying to hide the fact that you feel like shit from me?"

He laughed. "I'm better. Abigail is my past. I've let her go."

"That's good. Then what is it? Is there someone new?"

He raked his fingers through his hair and sighed. "It's complicated. There are two someones actually. I'm attracted to and starting to have feelings for both of them."

"Well, who makes you the happiest?"

"That's just it. I don't know if the woman who I could probably be with is even interested. And I don't think I could ever really be with the one interested in me."

"You've been hurt before by trying so hard to make a relationship work. Maybe this time, don't try. If it is meant to be, it will be. Just follow your heart and see where it leads you. But you have to be honest with those women. No relationship can start with deception."

"You always know what to say."

As soon as he hung up, another call came through. He answered the unknown number.

"I need to talk to you. I just ended it with Hugo, and I fear we may have made a mistake." Abigail's voice irritated him to no end.

"You and Hugo?"

"No. You and I."

"I can't do this right now. I'm in the middle of something."

"What I have to say can wait until we can speak in person. You can reach me at this number to set up a time."

He wanted to say—Look, Abigail, we didn't make a mistake. In fact, I've never felt better to be free from the relationship that was always entirely too much effort for both of us. Take care of yourself. Best of luck. Cheers. But instead, something entirely different came out of his mouth, "Okay, I'll ring you later." He was a circus act, trying to juggle three women.

Chapter 9

Graham knocked on Hallie's door. He'd left yesterday without so much as a good-bye, but he'd called her an hour earlier and asked to meet with her. She'd agreed, and now here he was. A glutton for punishment. Hallie opened the door and walked outside. She wasn't in a dress, but her tiny shorts were just as provocative.

She patted her messenger bag. "I'm ready."

He relaxed; relieved she didn't ask him inside. Probably better if they stuck to public places from now on. "How about we go back to the B and B? I have a feeling Mrs. Brown wasn't telling me something."

"If you think the B and B has answers, let's go."

The only sound as he drove was the wipers on the windshield. The awkward silence was too much. "How are you liking London?"

"It's wonderful. The weather is crazy, but the history and atmosphere make up for it."

"It's a great place to live. Really live."

"Have you ever been to Washington, D.C.?"

"No."

"You should someday. There's a national cherry blossom festival every spring. It's breathtakingly beautiful. And D.C. has some of the best museums in the world, the Smithsonians among them."

"Your eyes light up when you talk about museums."

The corners of her mouth turned upward. "I've been told that before."

"Why did you decide to come to London before you started your career?"

"It was always the plan. Something I needed to check off my list before my adult life could really begin."

Graham nodded and focused on the wet road. He shouldn't be disappointed or hurt by her comment, but he was. For him, the opposite was true—his life hadn't really begun until he moved to London. The last seven years may not have been perfect, but there was a sense of belonging when he made England his home.

• • •

Mrs. Brown insisted she knew nothing more of the journals. Hallie didn't buy it. She booked the last available room. Call it a sixth sense ... the woman was hiding something, and they were going to get to the bottom of it.

Graham pulled her aside. "What are you doing?"

"Trust me. This is the only way to find out if Mrs. Brown knows more than she is letting on." The fact that there was only one bed didn't matter since they weren't actually planning on spending the night. Good thing ... one room, one bed with a man she was more than attracted to could be asking for trouble. The tension between them was palpable. And it wasn't just about the journals or ghosts. Would she be able to be in the same room with Graham and not feel the heat between them? She closed her eyes. His crooked grin gave her butterflies, so probably not.

The decor reminded her of a medieval castle. Walls adorned in a rich plum paper surrounded a canopy bed covered with a golden velvet quilt. Large mahogany nightstands flanked the bed. A wine-colored settee was positioned in front of the arched window. Three tall pillar candleholders stood beside the seating.

"I feel as though I've gone back in time," she said.

"The room I stayed in before wasn't as regal but had the same Old World feel to it."

She sat down on the settee and removed the journals from her bag. Graham moved beside her. She handed him the book and took a deep breath as she waited for him to read.

My dearest Edmund,

The air is thick with worry. I feel as though I have trouble breathing. You are all that keeps me sane.

Graham paused to turn the page.

My dearest Edmund,

I feel the strain of our anxiety in our lovemaking. If I had one wish, it would be to have never have heard the prophecy. Then, my love, I could spend every moment with you in pure happiness and not in trepidation. The thought crossed my mind to poison us both—that way we could at least defeat fate and die in each other's arms—but I can't bring myself to take your life or my own. Please forgive me for such thoughts. The sorrow of it all is torture.

Graham's voice strained as he read. Hallie tried to swallow the lump in her own throat. "This is so sad."

With an agreeing nod, he handed her the book.

My dearest Flora,

The same thought has crossed my mind as well, so no forgiveness is needed. My love for you is so profound; I have to believe it will reach you no matter where we may be. Call to me with your heart, and I will hear you.

"This is too much. Let's take a break." Dejected, Hallie placed the books back into her messenger bag.

"How about a walk around the grounds? The fresh air could do us both some good."

"Great idea." Hallie waited for Graham to lock the door and followed him downstairs to the outside. They walked along the greenery to the fishpond. Colorful flowers dotted the landscape. She paused to listen to a frog croak upon a lily pad. "It's peaceful here. I normally love the noise of the city, but today, the subtleness is nice."

Graham nodded as he stood next to her watching the fish create rings in the water. She couldn't help but notice the way the wind tousled his brown hair. He was such an attractive man. Just a little rough around the edges, which really only added to his looks.

"I'm sorry if I've disrupted your life."

He paused. "We should get back inside. See if we can find anything about the diaries anywhere."

They headed back to their room. As soon as they entered, a gust of cold air rushed passed them and knocked one of the candles off the pillar.

"What was that?" she whispered.

Graham walked over to the candle and positioned it back in its place. "It's fine, see?"

Hallie shivered. She went over to the messenger bag to find it empty. "The journals are gone!"

He rushed over. "What? Are you sure?"

"Yes." She held up her messenger bag. "I put them in here before we went outside."

"I'm sure they're in here somewhere."

"Someone stole them."

"No one even knew they were in there."

She rubbed her earlobe with a frown.

He searched the room. "Let's go tell the owner. We may have to file a police report."

"That's not going to help us with Flora and Edmund."

"We'll have to figure out another way."

They found Mrs. Brown in the kitchen. "Dinner will be ready in thirty minutes."

"We are not here about food. We need to report a theft."

The drop in her chin suggested surprise. "Theft?"

Hallie stepped up to her. "Yes. Three antique journals were taken from our room."

"Are you sure? We've never had a problem with that sort of thing."

Graham placed his hand on Hallie's shoulder. "We're sure."

"Oh my." She washed off her hands and dried them on a towel. "At the moment, I am the only one with the master key." She removed the key from her apron. "And obviously I've been in here cooking."

"Maybe the lock was picked," Graham offered.

"Let's take a look." They followed Mrs. Brown up to their room to examine the door knob. Nothing looked at all suspect, which was curious. "Are you sure you didn't just misplace them? It happens all the time. Just yesterday, a man thought he lost his phone and found it an hour later in his car."

Graham glanced at Hallie. "No, we're sure they were taken. We should call the police."

"Very well, please be discrete when talking to them. Rumors can hurt business."

"Curious they were the only things taken when my wallet was out in the open not three feet away."

Hallie narrowed her eyes. "Indeed."

"Can I still expect you two for dinner?"

"We'll be down."

Once Mrs. Brown was out of sight, Graham turned to Hallie. "We are going to search this place until we find them. I don't believe her."

"But why would she take something she sold to your uncle? It's not like she could resell them without you finding out."

"No one else knew about those diaries."

Cold air crept over her. She rubbed her arms in response. "Did you feel that?"

"Yes."

The lights flickered. Without hesitation, Hallie crashed into him. He held her tight. "Bloody hell."

"Do you think it's Edmund and Flora or some other ghosts?" she whispered.

"I don't think I can handle any more. I'm just now accepting the fact there may be two."

"I'm with you there."

Chapter 10

Much to his relief, the old locks opened easily with his credit card. It didn't say much for the security of the place, but he was happy to be able to search for the diaries. Graham grinned at Hallie as he opened the door to the top floor room he believed to be Mrs. Brown's. Ghosts, stolen diaries, secrets. He wasn't getting any closer to figuring out this mess than the last time he'd spent with Hallie.

He searched cabinets and under clothes in the dresser. Nothing. Maybe it was for the best. Hallie had more of a hold on him than he cared to admit. After what he went through with Abigail, he should hang his head in shame.

"I don't see them. We'd better hurry before someone sees us breaking and entering."

"Right." He relocked the door.

They headed down to the dining room for dinner. Graham couldn't help the suspicions he had about not only Hallie but now Mrs. Brown also. He pulled out Hallie's chair for her.

"Thank you."

He sat across from Hallie and kept an eye on the B and B owner as she mingled with the guests. She gave no indication of guilt. Could Hallie have done something with the diaries?

He chewed his food as he studied his companion. "It'll be dark soon. What do you want to do?"

Hallie placed her napkin on top of the plate. "I'm not leaving without my journals."

Not sure if it was wise to spend the night with the woman he couldn't trust but desired more than all the antiques in London, he nodded.

They barely spoke as they headed up to their room. "We should turn in early. I want to get up before Mrs. Brown to check the kitchen. I can take the settee. You can have the bed." He needed to keep his distance from her before he did something he'd regret.

"Don't be silly. The settee is much too small for you." She grabbed a blanket and sat down on the less than comfy seat. "You take the bed."

"If you're sure."

Still clothed, she curled up with the blanket. "I am."

He turned off the light and slipped under the smooth sheets. Eyes wide open, he stared into the darkness. He wasn't about to get any sleep. The last thing he needed was to have one of his sexual dreams with Hallie not even six feet away.

• • •

"What was that?" He must have drifted off, and now Hallie was standing over him with her cover wrapped tightly around her.

"What? And why is it so bloody cold in here?"

"I keep seeing orbs of light hovering in the corner of the ceiling."

He tried to focus in that direction. "I don't see anything."

"This is starting to creep me out." As she sat down next to him on the bed, one of the candles lit itself, casting flickers of light through the frigid room.

"Did you see that?"

She moved closer to him. "I saw it. Edmund, Flora, is that you?"

Graham swallowed the lump in his throat. It was one thing for him to see a sexy ghost in his sleep—it was another thing entirely for one to be haunting their room. He stood up and went over to the light switch. Before he could turn it on, the candle went out. Hallie let out a whimper.

Graham's cell rang, startling Hallie and causing her to jump into his arms. The softness of the body against him made awareness surge through him. He sucked in a deep breath and turned on the light. "It's just my phone."

She quickly let go of him and nodded.

"Abigail, it's the middle of the night."

"I know. I'm outside your room. The owner let me in."

He looked at Hallie and cringed, then turned to the door. "Why are you here?"

"We never got to finish our conversation. I waited for you to call me back, but you never did."

"How did you find me?"

"I never deleted the app on my phone."

"It's not a good time."

Hallie watched him pace. He sighed. "Hold on, I'll be right back."

"You're going to leave me alone? In here? With the ghosts?"

"Fuck." He opened the door to his ex.

She walked into the room and glared at Hallie. "You have company."

"Did you doubt that I would? It is a B and B, and as I said, it's not a good time."

Hallie crossed her arms. "We're not ... you know."

Abigail's glare intensified.

Graham raked his fingers through his hair. "It's none of her business. We're divorced."

Hallie walked over to the window, putting some space between them. The situation couldn't have been more awkward. He almost wanted to ask Flora if she were still here as well.

"What is so important that you tracked me down in the middle of the night?"

She took his hands. There was no spark, no warmth the way he felt when Hallie or Flora touched him. "As I said before, I think we may have made a mistake. When I started seeing Hugo, it was great a first, but then, I couldn't stop thinking about you and how I felt when we first met."

He pulled away from her. "We tried. We did. I wanted things to work with you. And when you called, for a moment, I thought we could try again. But now that you are here standing in front of me, I'm certain we made the right decision. We are not good for each other, Abigail. You have to see that."

"I shouldn't have come. I'm sorry, Graham. You can have your car back."

"Keep it."

The lights flickered. His ex hugged him and walked out the door.

He placed a hand on Hallie's shoulder. "I'm sorry you had to witness that."

"It's fine. I'm sorry your marriage didn't work out."

• • •

She shouldn't be happy Graham turned away his ex, but relief had washed over her when Graham had told her it was over. When Hallie's body was in his arms, she had wanted to kiss him.

"The sun is about to come up. We should go check out the kitchen before anyone wakes up. If you still want to."

She nodded. "Of course. The journals are still my top priority."

He led the way down to the lobby. Hallie could have sworn the swirl of cold air was following her, maybe even leading her. She rubbed her arms.

They entered the kitchen. Graham started pulling open cabinet drawers. Hallie was drawn to the pantry, as if Edmund was holding her hand, pulling her. She went right to a large sack of flour and uncovered the missing journals as if Edmund had led her there. She grabbed them and rushed out the door to Graham. "I found them."

"How did you know where to look?"

"I think Edmund led the way. As soon as I picked them up, the cold dissipated."

He gave her an odd look. "So Mrs. Brown did take them. It's time to find out what that woman is hiding. I don't like secrets and hidden agendas."

If Hallie didn't know any better, she'd think that statement was meant for her and not for the B and B owner. "Neither do I." She clutched the journals to her chest.

Mrs. Brown stepped into the kitchen. "Breakfast isn't for another hour."

Graham crossed his arms. "We're not here for breakfast. Do you mind explaining why we found Ms. York's diaries in your kitchen pantry?"

The woman flipped on the light. "You're probably not going to believe me, but those diaries need to be destroyed. I always had my suspicions about them, but when you arrived, it only confirmed what I had feared all along. Those books are haunted."

Graham glanced at Hallie. "Why do you say that?"

"When I acquired them, odd things started happening here. Lights would go on and off by themselves. I even had an electrician check the place out to find nothing amiss. Items would be moved from where I knew I had put them. And temperatures would go up and down without my touching the thermostat. I sold the books to get rid of them. And as soon as they were off my property, things returned to normal. As if the diaries were haunting me to leave. You have no idea how relieved I was until you showed up asking about the very thing I had hoped to never have to deal with again. Still, nothing out of the ordinary happened until Ms. York came to stay here with you. The temperatures started going crazy. I could feel the little hairs on the back of my neck stand up. That is when I knew you'd brought back the haunted objects and that I would have to destroy them once and for all."

Hallie eyed the woman. "So why did you hide them instead of destroying them?"

"Oh, I tried. I set fire to them, but they would not burn. I even threw them in the duck pond, only to find them back on my nightstand dry as a bone."

Graham crossed his arms. "Did you ever read the diaries?"

"Yes."

"And what did they say?"

"Nothing really. Just ordinary and actually boring details about Big Ben."

"Did you ever come across the names Flora and Edmund?"

"No, why?"

"Never mind."

Hallie opened the books and flipped through them. "The pages are blank." She frowned and ran her fingers along the paper. Nothing. "Maybe you destroyed them after all."

"They weren't the last time I looked." She rubbed her arms. "If I did, trust me, I did you a huge favor. Now if you'll excuse me, I need to get breakfast started."

They took the collective works back to their room. Hallie flipped through the blank pages, and her heart saddened. She looked at Graham in question and then back to the wordless paper.

"Cry on it, like before."

Hallie nodded. She let the sadness take hold. She blinked and smeared her tears over the paper. Nothing happened. "I ... I don't understand. That's it? How are we supposed to help them without any further information?"

"I don't know."

Emptiness filled her chest. "I think I need some time alone."

Chapter 11

Hallie couldn't sit on the floor of her flat all day. She closed the journal and sighed. She grabbed her purse to call a cab. With the empty journals tucked inside her messenger bag, she headed downstairs. She stepped outside to wait for the cab. God, it rained a lot in London, and she still hadn't bought an umbrella. She didn't care. Her body was numb anyway. By the time she climbed into the car, rainfall had soaked her hair and clothing.

"Where can I take you?"

She spoke without thought. "Big Ben, please." Hallie blinked the water out of her eyes. She brushed her wet hair away from her face.

After paying the cabbie, she stepped out of the car in front of the monumental clock. Despite the weather, tourists scattered about the area. Hallie kept en route until she reached out and placed her hand on the clock tower. No visions came to her as before. Disappointment fell over her, as did the continuous rain. She sneezed and shivered. Since catching a deathly cold was not her intent, she turned to leave. About twenty steps later, Big Ben's chimes sounded. The scent of leather and amber filled her nose. Passion and desire once again ignited inside her, bringing her chilled body warmth.

She reached out into the air, not caring what people thought about her. His lips were on hers, his body molding to hers. She whispered, "Edmund, is that you?" An image of Frederick's aged face appeared. Time stood still. It couldn't be, could it? "Frederick?" Any sensation of his presence vanished. Chills slid down her spine.

• • •

Graham waited outside Hallie's flat, holding the red umbrella he'd bought her. Hallie York might not have the purest of intentions for him, but he had to find out the hard way. He was no stranger to heartache, and at least he wasn't entering whatever this was blindly.

She opened the door.

"I see you made it back … I thought you could use one of these." He handed her the umbrella.

She paused and tilted her head. "Thanks, I really need this."

He stepped inside and swallowed the lump in his throat.

She leaned the umbrella in the corner. "I went to Big Ben. Edmund has been appearing to me."

"Flora has been appearing to me."

She let out a nervous laugh.

"What do they want from us?"

She licked her bottom lip.

Unable to fight his craving any longer, he took a step closer to her and ran a finger along her cheek to her jaw.

She breathed heavy and tilted her chin up to him. "I don't know what they want, but I'm beginning to see what I want."

Graham captured her mouth in his. She matched the rhythm of his tongue. His mouth made love to hers. Brilliant. Sexy. Better than any kiss he'd ever shared, and just as intense as his fantasies of Flora. He ignored that last thought and let himself enjoy the realness of their touch. The more he kissed Hallie, the more the ache to do to her body what he was doing to her mouth grew uncontrollable. He took her hands and laced their fingers together.

Caught up in passion, they rushed up to her room. Hallie pulled off her top. He unfastened her bra, letting her spill out unrestrained. Her breaths, coming hard and fast, dizzied him with desire. Her nipples hardened further under his skillful fingers. Throbbing with want, Graham took off his clothes. To hell with reason and consequence. He bent her over the chair and pressed himself into her. Hallie tilted her neck as he caressed her offering with his tongue and lips. Not once did they remove their exploring hands from each other. He thrust into her from behind, cupping her breasts as he did. Their rhythm wasn't slow or sweet. It was demanding and wild, pent up desire on a mission to be released.

She turned to face him and pulled him to the mattress and on top of her. He held down her arms with his. Hallie cried out with release. When their birthmarks connected, something in her eyes grew possessive. Instead of scaring him away, it made him reach the peak of the mountain he'd been climbing. He pulled himself from her before he exploded. Relieved that he'd had enough self-control to remove himself from her in time, he relaxed into the mattress. Hallie awakened something deep inside of him. He just wasn't sure what.

She pressed her swollen lips to his. "You're incredible."

• • •

Graham stood in the shower, letting the hot water sluice down his back. Sex with Hallie was passionate and real. So why did he feel like he was cheating on Flora? Ashamed even. Like he still wanted something he couldn't have. She was a ghost or some psychotic fantasy. It wasn't like they could have any kind of actual relationship.

And God, did he want Hallie again. The woman was beautiful and intelligent. He wasn't ready to let Hallie go. Maybe he never would be. Something about her eyes tugged at his heart.

Graham shut off the water and dried himself on the thin towel. "What are we doing?"

She touched his lips before he could finish. "Let's just enjoy whatever this is for now. We can analyze it later."

He smiled and nodded. There would be plenty of time to talk, and at least maybe he could better sort out his feelings. Even though she'd given him no reason to believe she was out to get him or destroy him in any way, doubt crept into his mind. He relaxed his shoulders and took a deep breath. So he had trust issues. He'd have to work on that.

Chapter 12

Hallie rubbed her earlobe. Making love to Graham was amazing. And she wanted to do it again. Would she be ready to leave London when the time came? Maybe she could extend her stay if even a little. Her career may not allow it, and that saddened her. The passion between them was just as deep as what she'd felt with Edmund.

The lights flickered, reminding her that she wasn't finished. The ghosts were restless. She picked up one of the journals and opened it. Her fingers traveled the blank pages. She willed the ink to appear. But even her tears of frustration didn't make the written words come back. She threw the useless book across the room. "What am I supposed to do?" Cold air swirled around her, making her shiver. "Do you hear me?" The front door opened. She rubbed her arms and grabbed her purse. Damn rain. She grabbed the umbrella Graham had given her and made her way to McCoy's even though what she really wanted was a super-sized glass of wine at The Lion Den.

Graham opened the door with that slightly crooked grin of his. "Come in."

Hallie removed her jacket to distract herself from the desire building up inside.

He hugged her. "I guess we should have that talk now."

God, was he about to dump her? Maybe he'd gotten what he wanted, and now she was as worthless as the empty journals.

"I like you. A lot. But I need to tell you something."

Her mouth went dry. She clasped her fingers in front of her so he wouldn't see them shaking.

"This isn't easy to say out loud." He raked his fingers through his hair. "Flora has been coming to me in dreams. Intense sexual dreams. And I think I am in love with her."

A giggle slipped past Hallie's lips as the fear he was dumping her vanished. "I'm sorry. I don't mean to laugh at you."

"Bloody hell, I'd laugh at me too."

Hallie placed her hand on his arm. "Edmund has been doing the same thing to me. When it happens, I feel like he's the air I need to breathe."

"Why are they doing this to us?"

"I don't know. But we have no choice but to help them. They're restless, and restless spirits are never a good thing."

"How are we supposed to help them? And I'm confused. If they love each other so much, why are they having ghost sex with us?"

"There has to be a reason. I just know in my gut that if we can reunite those two, they will leave and we will be able to move on with our lives."

"Maybe, but why aren't the journals working anymore?"

"I don't know. I tried again before coming here. We can't rely on them to help us. We'll have to find another way."

• • •

"I want to make love to you again, but maybe we should wait until we figure out what these ghosts want from us, so things don't get any more complicated than they already are." He couldn't let himself be with Hallie again until this was over. It was the only way he'd know which of his feelings were real and what was manufactured by supernatural beings. The look of disappointment on her face was good for his ego but not his heart.

"I agree. In fact, I was going to tell you the same thing." The indifferent expression on her face was impossible to read. "I have an idea." She took out her phone.

Graham paced while Hallie talked to Madam Epiphany. From the sound of it, the woman refused to see them. Ever. Had the ghosts gotten to her? There had to be answers somewhere, but so far, every lead was a dead end. They needed to start over. Go back to the day he first saw the diaries. But he never put the diaries out for sale. Jane had.

He grabbed Hallie's hand and pulled her into the store. He eyed his employee as if seeing her for the first time.

Jane looked up from the vase she was cleaning. "What's happened?"

"Jane, it's really important. Where exactly did you get Hallie's diaries?"

Her hand went to her heart.

"Please, I need the truth."

"I'm so sorry, dear. I don't know what came over me, but I took the diaries from a hidden compartment inside your uncle's armoire and put them out. I didn't even know they existed until that moment. Then I lied to you about it. I'm terribly sorry. I honestly don't know why I did it. It was as if something was controlling me."

Hallie glanced at him. "Or someone. Do you think Flora and Edmund had her move the journals so I'd purchase them?"

The woman looked at the two of them as if they'd gone mad. "Who are Flora and Edmund?"

"Jane, you've been a trustworthy employee and friend. It's okay. I'm not mad at you, but I need you to show me the precise location where you found these."

"Of course."

They followed Jane downstairs to the massive armoire, where his assistant opened the door and moved the clothing aside. With one push, a hidden panel opened to what appeared to be an empty safe.

"Was anything else inside this safe other than the diaries?"

"Just a piece of your uncle's broken glass collection. I put that in the box with the others."

Graham picked up one of the milky white shards to examine it closer. Some sort of metal lined several of the fragments. "Thank you, Jane, we'll take it from here."

Hallie picked up another. "There had to be a reason it was stored safely away with the journals."

"We need to find answers."

"Grab the glass. We are going to pay Madame Epiphany another visit whether she likes it or not."

• • •

"I've told you all I can."

Hallie snatched the door to stop it from closing in their faces. "You've told us nothing. Please, what did you see the first time you saw us? You said that you saw excruciating pain. What exactly does that mean?"

The seer moved her toffee-colored curls away from her face. With a sigh, she waved them inside. Hallie and Graham took a seat at the round table across from a woman who was either crazy or the only person who could make sense of the madness that had become their lives. She paused as her eyes landed on Hallie's purse. Hallie, taking the hint, paid her. Immediately, the seer stared into her crystal ball and chanted. As the all-telling orb glowed, a tear slid down her cheek. "I see blood, lots of it. And broken ice, almost like white glass. And," she gazed at Graham, "your lifeless body."

Seemingly unaffected by her revelation of his death, Graham removed the large shards from his bag. "Like this?"

Madame Epiphany took one of the shiny fragments and held it in her hand. "Hard to say, but I do know this is sacred. It's important somehow."

"Can you tell us more?" Hallie pried.

"It's not that simple. I get bits and pieces, not an entire picture."

Hallie pulled more cash out of her wallet.

Madame Epiphany shook her head and slouched in her chair. "I'm exhausted. I must rest. I can tell you that many forces work against you and what you seek."

Hallie shivered, not from the seer's words but because of the actual temperature drop in the room.

"You must leave." Madame Epiphany flung her dark purple cloak around her and headed for the door.

Graham stood and took Hallie's hand. She liked the feel of his skin touching hers. What if the seer was right? Her heart fell.

Once they were outside, he turned to her. "Stop looking at me like that! Don't tell me you believed that bit about my impending death."

"I don't know what to believe."

"Maybe there is something to this broken glass. My uncle was peculiar, but I don't think he was mad. We should seek the help of a historian to learn more about the shards' meaning ... if they have one."

"You happen to know a historian?"

"Unfortunately, yes. My ex-wife's stepbrother is a history professor at King's College."

They had to follow any lead. "What are we waiting for?"

"It's better if I'm not the one doing the asking. The man hates me. Maybe you'd have better luck."

"What's his name?"

"Archie Breckenridge."

She tilted her head. "Archie won't know what hit him."

Chapter 13

Hallie pushed up her boobs before walking into the professor's empty room. She didn't normally use her body this way, but desperate times and all that.

"Professor Breckenridge, we spoke on the phone." She held out her hand with a you-may-get-lucky-if-you-give-me-what-I-want smile.

"Yes, Ms. York. Please, call me Archie." He motioned for her to have a seat next to his podium. He wasn't totally unattractive, but he was going bald and had a bushy mustache resembling a caterpillar.

She crossed her legs, knowing full well the slit of her dress would inch up even higher. "It's just so important I find out all I can about these pieces of glass."

"Let's have a look."

She handed him the box containing the mysterious shards.

"May I ask where you got these?"

"They belonged to someone very special to me."

"I can tell just by looking, this is pot opal glass. From the thickness and the cast iron on some of the pieces, I think I know where it's from. But before I let you in on my suspicion, I'll run some tests to determine the age and location from which it may have come."

"I'd be so grateful. Here's my number." She tossed him another seductive smile then swayed her hips as she exited the room.

Graham stood outside, leaning against the wall with his arms crossed. "Well?"

"We should know about the glass soon."

"I was right to send you."

Her stomach rumbled. "In the meantime, maybe we could grab a bite to eat. I'm starving."

"I could eat."

• • •

"Are you sure?" The room around her spun. She steadied herself against the wall. "You're certain the glass came from the face of Big Ben?" Her heart skipped a beat. This could be the connection in all the randomness.

"Yes, absolutely."

"Thank you." She ended the call and grabbed the red umbrella Graham had given her. The rain was steady but warm against her bare ankles. The back of her heel splashed in a puddle of water. A sudden craving for her mother's homemade chicken noodle soup took her by surprise. Uh-oh. The only time she wanted the hearty soup was when she was sick. She felt her forehead with the back of her hand to try to determine if she was coming down with something. Sort of clammy, but not hot. She squared her shoulders and continued on to Graham's.

By the time he opened the door, her extremities were weak. "Hi."

"Hi." She lowered the umbrella. "The opal glass, it's from Big Ben." She took a step and stumbled forward.

Graham caught her in his arms. "You're burning up!"

Illness always seemed to come at the most inconvenient times. "It's okay."

"Let's get you inside out of the rain. I'm not a doctor, but wet clothes can't be good for you if you're feverish."

She let him undress her down to her bra and panties. Since her body wasn't up for sex, there would be no temptation to break their agreement.

"You can rest in my bed."

Too tired and out of it to argue, she crawled under the covers, shivering.

"Can I get you anything?"

"No ... well, maybe another blanket." Her head hit the soft pillow. Nothing was ever so welcomed.

Graham tucked a quilt around her and kissed her forehead. Hallie snuggled deep into the covers and let sleep take her away.

• • •

Orange-red flames seduced the wood until it crackled. Warm, naked bodies intertwined on a white sheet next to the fire. Her hands traveled along his chiseled chest. She paused at his taut nipples. Her nose rested at the crook of his neck. She breathed in the leather and amber scent that was all his. The love in her heart was more powerful than anything she ever knew. He poured wine over her breasts and licked off the liquid, sending heat hotter than the fire down below her belly.

"Edmund," she whispered.

"Hallie."

"Edmund," she moaned.

"Hallie, wake up."

She forced her eyes to open. The room was only lit from the lamp on the nightstand next to the bed. There was no fire and no Edmund. But even in the dimness, she could see that she'd made a grown man blush.

"You were having a dream. A brilliant one, from the sounds of it."

Great, now it was her turn to blush.

"Anyway, I thought you should eat something. I made soup."

"You made soup?"

"Don't act so surprised. I can cook ... some."

The surprise wasn't that he could cook, but the fact that he'd made her the very comfort food she'd been craving.

He placed his cool hand on her cheek. "I think your fever is going down."

She tried her muscles. When she was convinced they worked, she pulled herself into a sitting position. "How long did I sleep?"

"Eight hours."

"I'm sorry I took over your bed. I can't believe I was out that long." She sipped a spoonful of surprisingly flavorful broth.

He sat on the edge of the bed as she ate. "I'm glad you're feeling better. So, do you want to tell me about that dream?"

She dropped the spoon into the bowl. "No. But what I do want to talk to you about is the glass. We need to take it to Big Ben. Maybe we have another piece of this seemingly endless puzzle."

"We can talk about that in the morning. I want to make sure you're completely recovered."

He was right. She should rest. It had nothing to do with the fact that she wanted to spend more time with Edmund in her dreams. "Okay, but you're not sleeping with me."

"No worries, I don't want to catch whatever it is you have," he teased.

• • •

Graham closed his eyes. He couldn't stop thinking about Hallie in the next room, in his bed. Her almost naked body between his sheets. Bloody hell. This wasn't supposed to happen. This all started out as him trying to expose Hallie as a fraud. Instead, he was falling for her. And since when did he believe in ghosts? Now. Now he did. And he wished they would just leave him alone. His eyes grew heavy, and he yawned.

He ran his fingers through Flora's soft hair. He went to kiss her, but her face was covered in blood. Her neck fell back. She was dead! He screamed and ran. He wanted to die. The pain of loss was too much.

"Graham, it's just a nightmare. I'm here."
He opened his eyes.
Hallie stood over him with a worried look.
"It was so real. The pain." His breath was visible as the temperature dropped.
"Come to bed. Hold me. I don't want to be alone."
He stood up and took Hallie's hand. He could have sworn an orb of light floated away before he climbed into bed beside her. He spooned her, letting the weight of her body calm him.

They swam in a pond. The sunlight glistened across the water. Flora flung her wet arms around his neck. Her embrace surrounded him. He was happy. Life was as it should be. A man's face caught him off guard, right before he said, "It will work. You must believe."

• • •

Graham awoke to an empty bed. Though the daylight proved he'd slept through the night, he was still tired. "Hallie?"
"That was some night." She walked into his bedroom, dressed and showered. "I don't know how much more of this emotional rollercoaster and haunting I can handle."
They were in agreement. "I'm glad to see you're feeling better. What do you want to do?"
"I think we should take the glass to Big Ben. See where it leads us, if anywhere."
"That's fine with me, but the Elizabeth Tower is not open to the public. Maybe you can persuade Archie to get you a key."

He got out of bed, not bothering to hide the erection under his boxers. He wasn't quite sure if Hallie or Flora was to blame.

"I'll call him now ... in the other room."

Graham showered and got dressed. He'd almost forgotten he had an antiques shop to run. Thank goodness for Jane. After a quick call to his employee, he met Hallie by the door.

"As much as I want the truth, I'm going to have to get back to business soon. Jane isn't feeling well. I'm afraid she may be coming down with what you had."

"Poor woman. Archie has agreed to get me into the tower, but only for thirty minutes."

"Hopefully, that's all we'll need."

Of course, Westminster was crowded as always when they arrived two hours later. As soon as Graham stepped out of the car, heat warmed his face. Almost as if he were walking into a fire.

"I don't suppose you feel that?"

Hallie gave him a cautious look. "The heat? I thought I was getting sick again."

"No, I feel it too."

He unlocked the door and they made their way up the spiral staircase. Hundreds of stairs left them both out of breath. Finally at the clock face, Hallie removed the glass from her bag.

"It's definitely a match."

When they got close to the light bulbs, a burst of excitement rushed through Graham's body, but it disappeared as fast as it came on. "Well, we're here. Now where are Flora and Edmund?"

"I don't know. Just for a few seconds, I thought they were here. But now I'm getting nothing."

He followed Hallie around the tower for another twenty minutes. While they learned about the history of Big Ben by reading the displays, that was about all they learned. Disappointment fell over him. "You promised Archie you'd have the key back in thirty minutes. We should go."

"Just another dead end. When I get home, I'll take another crack at the journals. We're missing something. We have to be. Otherwise, what is the point of all this?"

Her defeated look said it all. He almost missed his old life before the day he met Ms. York. "Meet me at The Lion Den at six? I think we could both use a pint."

"Okay. See you at six."

• • •

Hallie sipped on her latte. The journals sat open beside her, mocking her. She tilted her head back and gazed at the ceiling. Her chest filled with sorrow. They were so close. So why didn't it work? And even if they helped Edmund and Flora reunite, where did that leave her and Graham? Was this really her purpose for dreaming about London all her life? If so, the universe had a sick sense of humor.

She'd been here for almost three months and hadn't accomplished much of anything. Sure, she'd just gotten to explore the inside of the famous clock tower, ridden on a double-decker bus, walked along the River Thames, strolled through Chelsea, and even visited the British Museum, but her life and career back in D.C. were looking better and better, all except for the fact that she'd have to leave Graham.

Hallie placed her mug in the sink. Latte wasn't cutting it. Maybe she'd get to The Lion Den early. She paused at the door. The red umbrella leaning against the wall caught her eye. It really was a sweet gesture. Graham wasn't at all the ass she'd once thought him to be.

Deciding to make a detour, Hallie knocked on Madame Epiphany's door. When the woman didn't answer, she knocked harder and called out her name.

"She's gone."

Hallie turned to see a woman with spiked blonde hair and tattoos around her neck and arms. "Gone?"

"Yeah, she moved out a few days ago. Said the place was haunted. She was a bit bonkers, if you ask me."

Hallie nodded. "Thanks." As she made her way to the bar, she couldn't help but wonder if Flora and Edmund had driven the seer away. Tired of having more questions than answers, she entered The Lion Den. She pulled herself up to the gold bar. "White wine, please, and pour it in the biggest glass you can find."

The barkeeper grinned and nodded. Then the blessed man set a whole bottle of alcohol in front of her.

. . .

When Graham strolled in, Hallie gave him a weak smile. "Madame Epiphany moved. I stopped by to try to talk to her again, and her neighbor said she'd left a few days ago, because the place was haunted."

He tossed back his drink and shook his head. "What if we just do nothing?"

"What do you mean?"

"What if we ignore Flora and Edmund and start living our lives for us again?"

She let out a snort. "I can't do that. There's something I haven't told you." She paused remembering Frederick's face. "When I was a little girl, I had this imaginary friend. He told me all about London and how I belonged there with him."

Graham's face paled. "Bloody hell. Until you just reminded me, I'd forgotten about her. I, too, had an imaginary friend. Before she vanished, she told me that one day, I would be met with two paths. One path would lead me to my destiny and the other would cause me to lose myself." He raked his fingers through his hair. "I was only eight years old. I didn't understand. Then I forgot all about it."

"See, this is bigger than we thought."

He placed his hand over hers and sighed.

• • •

After tossing and turning most of the night, Hallie was a zombie when the phone woke her. With her head pounding and eyes still closed, she answered, "Hello?"

"It's Dad."

She rubbed her eyes and mumbled, "Dad?"

"Sorry I woke you."

Her head throbbed from her excessive wine consumption last night. "That's okay. I was just getting up." She cracked her eyes, daring to look at the sunlight peeking through the window.

"Are you having a good time in London?"

"Yes. It's been an adventure to say the least."

"I hope this means you're still coming back home." He chuckled.

"Can you ask me that again in a couple of weeks?"

"Oh, Hallie. Don't tell your mom that if she asks."

"Don't worry, Dad. I'll always find my way back. I won't desert you two."

"I know you won't. Well, I just called to check on you. But I have forty ungraded papers waiting for me. I'd better get going."

"Me too. Thanks for calling. Send Mom my love."

She dreaded telling her dad something she knew he didn't want to hear, but she couldn't lie to him. She had no idea if she would return to D.C. at the time she'd originally planned.

Chapter 14

Graham had just finished with his final customer for the day when the phone rang. "McCoy's Antiques. We specialize in rare personal items."

"Mr. McCoy?"

"Yes?"

"This is Harriet Brown. I'm afraid I wasn't completely honest. I need to share something with you."

"What is it?"

"Well, my husband's great-grandmother's name was Catherine. But after you asked about the name Flora, it sounded familiar, so I did some digging in our family history and discovered Catherine's mother's name was Flora. I apologize for not telling you, but to be quite honest, this whole thing has me terrified. With the ghosts and all. I'm an old woman who lives alone—well, except for my guests—and I can't handle any more of this."

"So why are you telling me this now?"

"There's more. I didn't just sell your uncle the diaries. I also sold him some broken glass. Catherine had it in a box along with the diaries. When you didn't ask about it, I assumed it was long gone, but it's not." She paused. "The glass is back here in my garden."

"What? That's impossible. Hallie has it."

"No. I'm afraid not. Look, I don't want the glass here, and we both know what happens when I try to destroy something that doesn't want to be destroyed."

"Have the ghosts been back?"

"No, nothing unusual except for the broken white glass showing up. And I want to keep it that way."

• • •

Two weeks later, Graham sat next to Hallie inside Lovely Café. He took a bite of the best almond scone he'd ever eaten. "This is delicious."

Hallie playfully bumped her knee on his. "I told you."

They'd agreed to have a bite to eat and relax before talking about Flora and Edmund anymore. The break was welcomed and needed. He took his time chewing the last bite.

Hallie licked her lips, sending a burst of heat through him. What if they never got rid of the ghosts and he couldn't make love to Hallie again before she left? He pushed that unbearable thought out of his head.

She sighed. "It's gotten worse. Every time I see a bird, my birthmark tingles."

"Mine too. Have any more entries shown up in the diaries?"

"No. I still don't understand why. The ghosts are persistent in staying in our lives, but they are not making it clear why."

"Let's take a walk."

He took her hand as they strolled down the pavement. The sun was actually shining today, and Hallie couldn't have looked prettier. "How about we skip Big Ben and go to the museum?"

Her face lit up. "Really?"

"Really. I think we've earned a day for us." Graham looked down as his foot kicked something. A shard of glass. If only ghosts could talk.

• • •

Graham shook his head. "Look around you! Are we any closer to finding out what those bloody ghosts want than we were the day you showed me those fucking diaries? You only have a week left in London. Do you really want to go back home without at least getting on the London Eye?"

Frustration overwhelmed her. "I'm afraid of heights, so that was never part of my plan."

"You can't leave London without that experience."

She shrugged. She'd had more experiences than she'd cared to. "Sure I can."

"Do you trust me?"

"Yes." She did, more than she ever thought she would.

Her heart pounded. The observation wheel was just so high. She trembled and struggled to catch her breath. Graham held her tightly. They hadn't been this close since they'd slept together. The way his body molded to hers melted all her fears away. Even with the disagreements and frustration. Graham gave her little breathless moments she'd cherish forever. She was in love with the man, but the ghost that haunted her would not go away. She couldn't have a life with Graham or Edmund. Tears blurred her vision.

London hadn't given her clarity. London had broken her.

• • •

"So that's it? You're leaving right on schedule as if none of this ever happened?"

Her throat burned from the tears she held back. She placed the red journals in her bag and zipped it up. They belonged in a museum exhibit, not human hands. "We were caught up in something. Something unnatural. For God's sake, we think we are in love with ghosts! How can that be healthy? How can we ever have a normal relationship with each other? I think it's best we just put all this behind us. Try to move on with our lives. If the ghosts won't leave us behind, we have to try to leave them."

"Bloody hell, if you walk away from me, Hallie, that's it." The hurt and anger in his eyes were evident.

"It's the way it has to be. For both our sakes." She didn't want to end things this way. But for things to actually end, she had to. They had both wasted too much time already. She couldn't do it any longer. She had a life's plan to follow, and staying in London was never a part of that plan. Somehow, her search for fulfillment had left her more lost than ever. She had to snap out of it before her life spiraled even more out of control.

"Does it even matter that I care about you? That I don't want you to leave?"

Hallie pulled her suitcase to the door. "Good-bye, Graham."

"You're no different from my ex." He walked out of the flat, slamming the door behind him. The red umbrella fell to the floor with a thump.

Hallie sat down on the floor and cried until she had no more tears.

<h1 style="text-align:center">Chapter 15</h1>

At the Smithsonian, Hallie pried open the small wooden crate. She dug through the packing and removed a box that contained a bracelet that Napoleon had given to his second wife. The bracelet was only a myth until she'd proven it existed. The workmanship was exquisite, and it would join the rest of the Napoleon jewels in the Gem Gallery. She should have squealed the moment she saw the precious piece. Nothing excited her anymore. Not even having worked at the museum for a month or moving into her own apartment.

Ever since she'd left London—well, Graham really—she couldn't seem to find joy in anything. Or even focus. From all the way across the ocean, the man still had an effect on her. Edmund had left her alone, but in a strange way, it was Graham who haunted her dreams now.

After cataloging the artifact, she set out to meet her parents for dinner. She'd been avoiding them and their endless questions ever since she'd returned to D.C. But since it was her mom's birthday, she had no choice but to face them.

She drove straight to the Italian restaurant her mom had chosen. The greeter took her back to the table where her parents were already seated.

They stood up the moment they saw her. She walked over to her mom and hugged her. "Happy birthday. Did you get the flowers I sent?"

"Yes, thank you. They were beautiful. White roses are my favorite."

Hallie nodded and walked over to her dad. He brought her in for a tight embrace. "Great to see you finally."

Once seated, Hallie took a drink of her water. After a few moments of awkward silence, her dad was the first to speak. "You're different."

Her mom placed her hand on her dad's arm. "Jim."

"Well, she is. What is going on with you? Is it your job?"

"No. My job is great." She paused while the waitress set the baskets of garlic breadsticks on the table.

"Then what? You've always been honest with us. You miss London, don't you? You want to move there? Just tell us. We're all adults here ... we can handle it if our only daughter wants to live across the ocean."

Her mom shook her head. "Jim, that isn't helping. What he means is, we love you and will support you, no matter what."

Hallie choked on her breadstick. "It's not that." How in the world could she explain that she left things unresolved, not being able to help two ghosts find each other? Or that the man she'd left behind was all she could think about? She swallowed. "There was a man. We parted ways on bad terms. I have some regrets, that's all. I'll be fine once this passes." If it ever did.

"Hallie, you've been home for a month. Have you tried calling the guy?"

The image of the slamming door and the red umbrella falling to the floor popped into her head. "I've considered it, but it would just be a bad idea."

The waitresses brought hot plates of food to their table. Her mom smiled. "I hope you don't mind, I went ahead and ordered your favorite."

Her dad snorted. "If it still is her favorite."

She cocked her head to the side and sighed. "Yes, I still love chicken parmigiana." Even though she'd suddenly lost her appetite, she forked a bite of cheese-covered meat and shoved it into her mouth.

The waiter came to the table, holding an expensive bottle of wine. "Excuse me, the gentleman at the bar has sent this over."

Hallie turned to look. Her heart soared. Graham was sitting not even ten feet away. He waved with a smile. As if no time had passed, all the feelings she had for him came flooding back. Butterflies danced in her stomach.

"Darling, you're flushed. Do you know that handsome man?"

"Yes, Mom. I do. His name is Graham, and we were just talking about him."

"Well, what are you waiting for? Go to him. It seems you have some unfinished business."

Hallie nodded, but before she could get up, Graham strolled over.

"Sorry to interrupt."

Her dad stood up and shook his hand. "I'm Jim, Hallie's father."

"Graham McCoy. Hallie's ... friend from London."

"And I'm Hallie's mother, Adele."

"So nice to meet you both."

Hallie gulped down her wine. "What brings you to D.C.?"

"I came to the States because I owed my sister a visit and decided to stop off here before returning to London. Someone once told me how beautiful it is."

Her quick alcohol consumption put Hallie at ease. "Mom, Dad, can you please excuse us?"

"Of course. In fact, just call me tomorrow." Her mom winked.

Her dad nodded.

Hallie grabbed her purse. "Happy birthday." Her legs wobbled as they walked outside. They stopped on the busy sidewalk.

Graham stroked her cheek. "I'm sorry. The way we left things ..."

Desire rushed through her. "I'm sorry too. I've missed you. How did you find me?"

"I hope you don't mind, but there is this app on my phone. I kind of tracked you."

"I probably should." She grinned. "But I don't mind at all."

His mouth claimed hers, making her weak enough to fall into his strong arms. When they stopped for air, she looked into his eyes. "What does this mean for us?"

"If you want there to be an 'us,' we can figure something out."

She'd already made up her mind the moment she saw him again. "I'm sure I could get on at the British Museum."

"Really?"

"Really. I belong there. I've always known that deep down. I haven't had any visions of Edmund since I left you that day."

He cocked his head. "I haven't had any dreams about Flora."

"I'm certain I want you and only you. Ghosts or no ghosts, it's you that my heart beats for."

He cupped her face. "I feel the same."

The smile on her face came from deep inside. "Go get your bags from your hotel. You're staying with me until I can make arrangements to join you back in London."

He let go of her and stepped off the sidewalk, happier than she'd ever seen him. Before Hallie knew what happened, a car hit Graham from behind. The cab screeched as Graham lay limp on the pavement, blood pooling around him. Her screams echoed through the crowd gathering around her.

She fell to her knees as she heard someone scream to call 9-1-1. "Graham! Don't leave me. Please. Please." Tears blurred her vision. Her breathing came out in gasps. Excruciating pain seared through her heart. A vortex of darkness swooped her up and swallowed her whole.

• • •

Hallie's mom took her hand. "It's going to be okay. You're okay. You gave us quite a scare."

Her dad patted her hand. "Welcome back."

Hallie's mouth was bone dry. She looked around the tiny ER room where a nurse stood over her. "Graham."

The woman gave her a small smile. "He's in surgery. You're going to be fine."

"What happened? Why am I so sore?"

"You don't remember?"

Panic whipped through her. "I remember a car hitting Graham and ..." A tear slid down her cheek. "And all the blood."

Her dad placed his hand on her shoulder. "You fainted. I scooped you up, put you in the cab, and we followed the ambulance to the hospital. They took Graham and brought you in here."

Her mom kissed her head. "You should rest. I'll wake you as soon as we get news about Graham."

Tears blurred her eyes. Madame Epiphany's vision had come true. "I can't rest. Not until I know he's okay."

The nurse took her vitals. "Other than the nasty bump on her head, she'll be fine."

Another nurse came in. "I'm glad you're awake. Your friend is going to be fine. He pulled through surgery without any complications. It will take him some time to heal, but there shouldn't be any permanent damage."

"I need to see him."

"He's in Room 19. Third floor."

"Do you want us to go with you?"

Her mom grabbed her arm. "No. I need to see him alone. I'm fine. I'll call you when I get home."

After hugging both her parents good-bye and reassuring them she was fine, Hallie walked down the hall to the elevators. She stepped inside, her knees a bit weak. Thank God Graham would be okay. She couldn't lose him. Not now. As she entered his room, he turned to her.

"I heard you fainted."

She placed her hand over his and glanced at the monitor showing his vitals. "I thought I'd lost you forever."

"I'm not that bloody easy to get rid of." He let out a strained laugh.

"My mom called your sister. She couldn't make it here to see you but has been getting updates from your nurse."

"I know I just spoke with her."

She squeezed his hand and gazed into his eyes. "When I thought I lost you, without telling you how I feel, I wanted to die." She paused to swallow the lump in her throat. "I don't want to exist without you. You are the void that has always been in my heart." She kissed him gently, then deeper. "I love you."

"I love you. And I need to show you something." He reached under the sheet and pulled out one of the journals."

Her eyes widened. "How did that get there?"

"When I just told you, I love you, I felt it materialize under my hand." He opened it.

Hallie took a deep breath when the words appeared. She read, "You shall both die before you're meant to leave this earth. Because your love is so profound, the universe will throw your restless spirits back together many times. Your bodies will not be the same, so you will not identify each other. You will relive this agonizing destiny over and over unless your hearts recognize each other, and become one again."

Hallie gazed into Graham's eyes. And then it happened. Flora and Edmund appeared holding hands. Then with a bright light filling the room, their souls entered Hallie and Graham. The moment she was whole, Hallie recalled the seer from long ago using old magic to bury memories so deep that any amount of rebirth wouldn't totally erase them. Then he tattooed matching doves on their wrists so that they might recognize one another, though he warned the marks might not show up when they were reborn. They had though, in another form ... their birthmarks.

Big Ben's meaning was clear—Edmund had been a gasman and lit the lamps, which illuminated the four clock faces, every night. He'd watch over the lights until dawn to make sure they stayed lit. Flora would help him, and then they would make love under the flickering flames. He'd given her the extra broken pieces of pot opal glass he'd found as a memento of their special place.

She saw the fountain pen in her own hand as she scrolled entries into the red journals. She wore a Victorian nightdress the first time she felt the life drain from her. Then every life she'd spent lost without her love flashed before her eyes. It was clear why she'd been unfulfilled in this life.

She recognized his scent. Edmund. Her heart filled with more love than she ever thought possible. "Did you see? Can you ..."

"I did and I can. You smell like the finest sweet confection with a hint of earthy salt."

Pure joy lit her up from the inside. "We're them. They're us." She squeezed his hands. "Flora and Edmund and all the others that came after."

He nodded. "I believe it without question to be true."

Such transparency made her sigh with relief. "We're reincarnated."

"You're more than my destiny—your love has followed me through time and circumstance. You are what makes me, me. And I, you. A name is just a name. A body is just a body. All the pain that has brought us to this moment, the moment of clarity, has been worth it. Some men love with their heart, some with their mind. I love you with every molecule of my being and will through this life or the next. Our hearts have been reunified." He caressed her cheek.

She took her gaze away from his eyes, only to kiss him again. A long, sweet kiss edged with enough passion to last her a lifetime and more. Her heart soared. Recognition of who she really was gave her the fulfillment she'd always longed for. When she looked back at him, tears of happiness filled both their eyes. "How is it possible to love someone so much? Is this even allowed?"

"Bloody hell, does it matter?" He laughed. "Rules don't apply to us. We just ... are."

She nodded with a smile. Their hearts had become one. They wouldn't relive the prophecy any longer. The bliss of their everlasting love was worth any amount of pain. Hallie laced her fingers with Graham's and took a deep breath. They were together at last, and she was ready for eternity.

Acknowledgments

I thank God for giving me the determination and creativity to write. And my husband for the inspiration.

About the Author

Christy Newton is a hopeless romantic and writes many genres of romance. She just might be the only author out there who doesn't drink caffeine, but dark chocolate is her must-have. She falls in love with each of her heroes and hopes you will too! Christy lives in Indiana with her loving husband and two amazing daughters. She is the author of more than ten novels. Learn more about her at www.christynewton.com, on Facebook https://www.facebook.com/pages/Christy-Newton/359791990763912, and on Twitter @CNewtonAuthor.

Naturally Enchanted
Christy Newton

"We've been over this. I don't need herbs to find my *konpayon nanm*." The Creole word for soul mate rolled off Ezra Ravenhart's tongue. "I need the perfect man for that. One who is smart, charming, funny and—" She paused to purse her lips. "Sees me for who I really am. One who probably doesn't exist."

Grana smirked and shook an emerald-bejeweled finger at her. Ezra couldn't remember a time seeing her without the heirloom ring. A beaded silver comb held her long, pure white hair up in a loose twist. "Sometimes fate needs a little push, and don't ever underestimate the power of herbs."

"I wouldn't dare." A warm, floral breeze tickled the strands of beads hung in the doorway, sending a cascade of color throughout Mystic Herbs. With a smile, Ezra removed the small bottle of catnip from the lowest wall shelf. As she turned around, an anxious sensation accompanied by a sudden burst of energy took her by surprise. The bottle slipped through her fingers and, even though the glass didn't break, most of the greenish-brown herb ended up scattered over the countertop.

"I didn't mean to get you all worked up."

Ezra removed a paper towel from the drawer. Still a bit shaken, she funneled the herb back into the container. "I'm not worked up. The lid wasn't on." After putting a scoop of catnip inside a white paper bag, she carefully corked and placed the bottle back in its place among the hundreds of colorful aromatic plants contained in clear glass and lining the shelves.

Grana's aqua blue eyes lit up as she put her hands on her hips. "Mmm hmm. A little love vine wouldn't hurt."

"Good night, Grana. See you tomorrow." She'd just turned twenty-one and Grana was already afraid Ezra would end up an old spinster. Okay, there was some reason for Grana's fear. Except for her best friend, Piper, Ezra had spent much of her life alone. She'd filled her free time studying herbs in the garden or exploring the Forbidden Caves close by.

Mostly she'd kept to herself, because people thought Grana was a witch. They even accused her of mixing her herbal remedies in a cauldron. Of course Grana was a little eccentric and could do things with herbs no one else on the island could, but that wasn't witchcraft. It was pure skill. And she was almost positive Grana didn't own a cauldron.

Just because every Ravenhart woman had been a brilliant herbalist didn't mean they were witches. She rolled her eyes. It didn't matter. Let them think what they wanted. She'd learned long ago that Mango Cove Island was full of superstitious people, but Ezra wasn't one of them. She saw the island for what it really was—a beautiful hidden paradise nestled in the North Atlantic.

Ezra stepped over an iguana nibbling on a ripe fig—a common sight, lizards outnumbered people on Mango Cove. Sweet, humid air stuck to her skin as she shuffled past the bright pink hibiscus along the gravel path. The ruffled hem of her coral, lacy dress caught in a gentle wind and flittered against her thighs. She walked a quarter of a mile before she reached her small bungalow on the east side of Grana's property. Their ancestors were some of the first inhabitants, so Grana owned more land than most.

Ezra made her way up to the seafoam-green colonial style house trimmed with white shutters, one of many vibrant homes that lined the outer ridge of the boomerang-shaped island. The majority of houses were oceanside, too, and hers was no exception.

She removed her key from her straw handbag. Pops of her favorite color welcomed her in the living room where orange pillows, rugs and art were forefront to sand-colored walls.

Ezra looked around and shook the bag of catnip. "Mr. Sugar, I brought you a treat."

The white, short-haired kitty didn't make an appearance. Sure enough, she found the cat curled up in his favorite spot next to the back door on the sun-warmed tile. Clearly a stray, he'd wandered into her yard on her birthday a couple of days ago. From the moment she saw him, she knew he was meant to be hers. He'd taken well to living indoors and was no trouble at all. Grana had always told her to be patient and a special pet would show up in her life one day, when she'd begged her for one growing up.

Ezra went over to the natural wooden cabinet that held Mr. Sugar's special plate and took it out. With a grin, she sprinkled the attractant onto the ceramic dish and set it next to him. His amber eyes cracked open. It didn't take long before he was purring and rubbing his entire body in the herb.

Ezra laughed and leaned back against the paprika-painted wall. "You're welcome." She scratched his head. "Hey, what happened to your new collar?" Maybe she hadn't fastened it all the way when she'd put it on this morning. It must have fallen off. Her stomach growled, so she dismissed the missing collar and grabbed a pot of seafood gumbo, then a can of Cove Punch from the white refrigerator. Grana had warned her that Cove Punch was no good for her body, but the sugary, pineapple-flavored carbonated drink was Ezra's addiction. She'd had to smuggle in the cases of soda without Grana knowing to avoid a lecture. Sometimes Grana still treated her as if she were a child.

She took a long, refreshing drink and turned on her flat-screen TV that set on the countertop next to the white stove.

She simmered and stirred the thick soup while watching the local news. A story about a small unregistered boat being wrecked on the island without any passengers found aboard caught and held her attention. Their little island didn't get a lot of tourists. The wooden spoon in her hand stilled. She forgot to stir the gumbo and almost burned dinner. Something about the news of the abandoned boat gave her another anxious sensation.

• • •

"You don't think anyone saw me sneak into the inn last night?" Still feeling a bit seasick, Owen Cooper dug his fingers through the heavy, wet sand. He lifted a big blob and wiped his hands on his khaki shorts, then messed up his hair. The sand dried fast in the hot sun and stuck to him like gritty glue. He couldn't shake the anxious feeling he had from the moment his feet hit beach.

"No, it was too dark." His best friend and co-conspirator, Jace, looked at him as if he'd lost his mind. With his stylish blond hair and slightly crooked nose, many women mistook Jace for an actor or model. Owen personally couldn't see it.

"Good. No turning back now. Ready for a witch hunt?" Owen had talked Jace into coming along by convincing him he was long overdue for a *tropical* vacation. His wealthy friend's last travels were to cold climates where he'd enjoyed snowboarding and skiing. As rich as his best friend was, Owen was just as broke and any vacation would be nice for him. Jace inherited a trust fund when he turned eighteen, while Owen had inherited a mountain of school loan debt.

"This is either going to ruin your reputation or jump-start your career. Sorry, bud, I still think you're crazy."

"You don't think I actually believe she's a spell-casting, broom-flying witch, do you?"

Jace raised an eyebrow in mock surprise. "If not, then what are we doing here? And why did I let you talk me into staging a boat wreck? Nice tip you gave that reporter by the way."

Owen smirked, rubbing his sand-dusted beard. "It doesn't matter what I believe. I just have to convince the general public of Chicago what her own community has always believed: that Maeva Ravenhart is a witch."

"In all seriousness, I've traveled the world and have never come across anyone remotely supernatural. I still can't believe you gambled your possible promotion on an anonymous email that should have gone to your spam folder and died in a cyberspace landfill."

"There was a great sense of urgency to that email with many intricate details … it's my job to sift through what's news and what isn't." The truth was he didn't know why he felt so strongly about the information or why he had gambled his future on it. He normally was not a risk-taker. He glanced around the highly vegetated area to be sure they hadn't been seen. On a mission, he ripped his T-shirt and made the scrap into a primitive sling for his left arm. "Do you think adding a limp is overkill?"

"I don't know. This is your scheme—I'm just here for the sun and the babes. I'm on vacation, remember?"

"Right." Owen paused. "A limp may be hard to keep up. I'll stick with the sprained wrist. Maybe add a concussion."

Jace shook his head. "You better hope that woman can't really turn you into a toad if she finds out what you're doing."

Owen laughed. "As much as people want to believe magic exists, I know it doesn't. But that doesn't mean I can't write a convincing enough story to make people question reality. Even if just a little." He pulled a map he had printed off the computer from his pocket. "Maeva Ravenhart's herb shop is about a mile south. I'll have to travel on foot. No one can see me if they are to believe I was shipwrecked."

Jace raked his fingers through his hair. "Good luck. I hear a cocktail calling my name. Not to mention that hot blonde in the pink bikini who just walked out of the inn."

"I'll catch up with you when I can." Owen took a deep breath of fresh, mildly salty air as he watched his friend wander to what would be another one of his conquests. He wouldn't be as lucky— his destination lay toward that thick cluster of palm trees and ferns. Squawks of tropical birds sounded overhead as he traveled along a gravel path. The rocks crunched beneath his sandals. Every ten feet he saw more lizards. He'd never seen so many iguanas in one place.

When the herb shop was in view, his adrenaline kicked into high gear. If he played his cards right, after he left Mango Cove, he'd be able to write any story he wanted from an office with a view. Maybe not as sweet as the view on the island, but the inside of a cubicle was no way to spend a hard-earned career.

He didn't scrape by to go to graduate school for the leftovers his boss tossed to him every now and then. Determination surged through his veins. His days of living off of ramen noodles were almost over. Owen had learned from some insider information that when his boss agreed to let him check out Maeva Ravenhart, it wasn't because he believed in the supernatural or rookie journalists … it was to get Owen out of the way. Budget cuts were every hard-working man's nightmare. That was the only push Owen needed to make sure he came back with the story of a lifetime. People always wanted to believe there was something more out there, anything to take them out of the boring reality that was their life. Soon he'd be the king of *The Chicago Post*. This was his chance to fast-track his career.

He made his way toward the lavender colonial style building. A colorful wooden sign confirmed he'd reached his destination. Mystic Herbs … even sounded like a witchy name. Various herbs tied with twine hung upside down on either side of the paneled glass door and sweet-scented yellow flowers bordered the shop. He stepped up to the first of three wooden steps, taking his time to appear wounded and confused.

"You're searching for something."

The voice from behind startled him. He turned around to face a woman with snow-white hair piled on her head, wearing a long, flowing dress the same color as the ocean. She'd come from out of nowhere. A large, oval-cut emerald ring circled her index finger.

"Yes, I—" If this was the woman he was looking for, she wasn't what he'd expected. Petite and, though aged, her face was still striking. She had high cheekbones, bright eyes, and a wisdom about her he couldn't explain. Not as he'd pictured an island witch to be but even better. Photogenic people sold stories.

She touched his sling-covered arm. He could feel the warmth of her fingers through the thin cotton fabric. With a slight tip of her head she looked into his eyes as if reading a book. It made him uncomfortable. A wind chime blew in an abrupt breeze, sending a melody out into the otherwise silent air. Tiny hairs prickled on his neck.

The woman removed her hand. "My granddaughter's inside. She can provide you with what you need." Before he could thank her she walked away, her dress fluttering behind her.

There could be some truth to those ancient rumors after all. *Nah.* Now he was being ridiculous, feeding into the story he'd been preparing in his head. She was just an elderly woman, the owner of an herb shop … nothing astonishing about that.

He opened the glass door, which triggered a bell. The inside of the shop was painted the color of rich honey, and bright white shelves held too many bottles of various sizes to count. The combination of the high counter, glass bottles, and apothecary scale reminded him of an old-time pharmacy. He skimmed some of the handwritten labels, which didn't include any bat wings or eye of newt, much to his relief and somewhat disappointment.

Owen turned his head to a small doorway separated by a curtain of multicolored, plastic gemstones. A petite woman dressed in pink with shoulder-length hair as black and shiny as polished onyx emerged carrying a granite mortar bowl and pestle. Her midnight-blue eyes gazed intensely at him as she set down the tools behind the counter. She had to be Maeva's granddaughter. Same high cheekbones, same concentrated stare. Her doll-like nose paired well with her flawless face.

When the peaches-and cream-skinned beauty didn't say anything, he cleared his throat. "I was hoping you'd have something to help me heal. I think I was in an accident, not far from here."

Her eyes went to his chest, then to the handmade sling. "You think you were in an accident or you know you were?"

"I, uh, I can't exactly recall." He looked down at his arm and winced. "I just know I need something for the pain."

"Of course. Welcome to Mystic Herbs." She caught her bottom lip in her sparkling white teeth and turned to the shelves. "I'm sure I have something."

He raised an eyebrow. "But you haven't asked me what's wrong."

She grabbed bottles of powdered turmeric and rosemary and came around the counter. "Well, your arm's not broken or you'd be howling out in pain." A light, floral fragrance combined with the delicious scent of coconut filled his nose.

For good measure, he groaned when she touched his arm. Her small hands worked their way around his muscles. Her touch was amazing. He fought to keep a smile from his face as she worked her way down to his wrist.

"Must be a sprain." She looked up into his eyes and jerked her hand away as if she hadn't realized she'd been massaging him. "Have a seat." She pointed to a dark purple wooden bench behind him. "I'll be right back."

He watched her walk away and couldn't help but notice her sexy legs in those incredibly tiny, hot pink shorts. Though her sheer, pale pink top was loose, it was just as seductive. She was petite and not especially curvy, but the important curves were definitely there. It wasn't just her body that made his blood pump harder though—the look in her intense eyes, as if she wanted to devour him, was just as potent.

•••

Ezra rushed through the beaded doorway and leaned her back against the wall to steady herself. She brought a quivering hand up to feel her out-of-control heart. The moment she'd laid eyes on the disheveled, rugged man, she'd felt a strong undeniable pull toward him. Almost magnetic and unlike anything she'd ever experienced.

She'd love to wash off that sand-covered skin of his in a nice hot shower. The sparse curls on his chest matched the hair on his gorgeous head. And when she touched his arm, even through the fabric, it took everything in her to keep from planting a kiss on his magnificent lips. His copper-blond hair was dusted with sand as were his close-trimmed beard and mustache. She licked her lower lip and bit it as she took a deep breath. A man had never affected her that way before, so that she could barely control herself. It was if she'd lost her mind or had been enchanted.

Nonsense … she didn't believe in such things. She inhaled another deep breath through her nose and exhaled slowly. Maybe Grana slipped some love vine into her tea this morning. She'd be fine when it wore off. She rushed over to the antique stove and heated a small amount of water to a boil. After she mixed the turmeric and rosemary with the hot water to make a paste, she went back out to the front room to face her uncontrollable desire sitting on the bench.

"I wondered if you were coming back." He looked around the shop. "What island am I on?" His head wobbled a bit.

Ezra rushed over to him. "You may have a concussion." She studied his eyes, which were almost as green as Grana's emerald. "Hmm, your pupils look fine. What happened to you? Do you know your name?" She had a hard time not gazing at his toned chest.

"I'm Owen and you are?"

She extended her hand. "Ezra Ravenhart, co-owner of Mystic Herbs. You're on Mango Cove."

He took her hand and just when she thought he was going to kiss it, he shook it instead. "I'm not sure what happened, but when I woke up I was lying on the beach next to my wrecked boat."

Her eyes widened. "I saw that on the news last night. The authorities found your boat, but where have you been since then?"

He cocked his head and narrowed his eyes. "I think I fell asleep under a palm tree. Maybe a coconut fell on my head."

Americans were so dramatic. "Doubtful, but you may have been in shock. I don't think you have a concussion, but you should get to the hospital for a checkup." She removed his soiled sling and examined his arm. It wasn't swollen or scraped. "I'll just put on some paste that I mixed for sprains. It'll help in no time."

He rubbed his dirty face. "Thanks."

She nodded and dipped her fingers into the turmeric remedy. "Now, where does it hurt?"

"My wrist and elbow. But before you do anything, I don't have any money. My wallet must have gotten swept off with the tide."

Poor man. Her teeth caught her lower lip. Poor, unbelievably sexy man. "That's okay." She rubbed the mixture on him, which turned out to be much too sensual. She turned her face away so he couldn't see the blush that must be rising to her cheeks. She'd almost moaned, for goodness sake. She was acting like she'd never been around a man before.

"That woman outside, who is she?"

She turned her head back to face him. "My grana. Her name is Maeva and she owns half of Mystic Herbs. She was the sole owner, until I followed her footsteps and became an herbalist. It's kind of a family tradition. The shop has been in our family for generations."

"Ezra … that's an unusual name for a woman."

She moved her fingers away from his muscular arm. "I was named after my granddad. He was lost in the Bermuda Triangle along with my parents. I was only two years old, so I don't remember any of them much. Although I do have this memory of building sandcastles and riding on my dad's shoulders with my arms wide in the air."

He frowned. "I'm sorry. That must have been hard growing up without parents."

She shrugged. "I never knew any different and I always had Grana." Great. Now she was she blabbing her family history to this stranger. She'd not really talked to anyone about her family before, except for Piper.

"The name suits you. You're different, I can tell." He grinned. "Ezra, Ezra, Ezra, has anyone ever told you that you are gorge—" He slumped over on the bench.

Just her luck. The man was about to tell her that she was gorgeous and he fainted before he could finish. Things never worked out for her in the romance department. She rushed over to the wall of herbs and grabbed a glass dropper. A few drops of peppermint and lavender oils would do the trick.

Grana returned as she was reviving Owen, the mysterious shipwrecked man her body seemed to want to fuse with. She narrowed her eyes at Grana. "You slipped love vine in my tea, didn't you?"

She raised a thin, white eyebrow. "I did no such thing."

Ezra pressed her lips together. "Grana."

"Your patient is waking up."

Ezra's heart sped up as his green eyes cracked open. "You fainted. You really should lie down."

Owen nodded. "Mango Cove, that's where I wrecked, right?"

He was still confused. He had no money and was in obvious trauma. She couldn't just send him on his way. She'd feel guilty if something were to happen to him. It had nothing to do with the fact she'd go crazy if he weren't close by.

"Yes, Mango Cove," said Grana.

Before Ezra knew what was happening, she piped up with her half-baked idea. "You lost your wallet and you need to rest. I think I have the solution. We have a guesthouse you can stay at for free, until you feel back to your old self." Grana and Owen looked as surprised as she felt. She really hadn't just offered a stranger to stay on their land, had she?

Owen's eyes sparkled in the sunlight. "Thank you. I appreciate that."

Her heart pounded inside her chest. She most certainly had.

Also by Christy Newton:

Begin Again:

"Newton['s] … knack for developing a strong hero and heroine whose love story, with its mild romantic scenes, quickly immerses the reader. A sweetly charming read." —*Library Journal*

"This story is great; it is not only about loss but also second chances … Two broken souls that will heal each other with care and a good friendship that will slowly develop into something more meaningful. A sweet and emotionally heartwarming read." —Harlequin Junkie

In the mood for more Crimson Romance?
Check out *His Lass Wears Tartan by Kathleen Shaputis* at
CrimsonRomance.com.